8/11/05

Elizabeth –

All of these stories
are true, but also
not true.

Alvin

OUT FAR IN DEEP

Short Stories by Alvin Handelman
with graphics by Sharon Brown

Minnesota Voices Project Number 39

NEW RIVERS PRESS 1990

Three of the stories in *Out Far, In Deep* have appeared in somewhat different versions in the following publications: "Provide, Provide" and "The Fall" appeared in *Twin Cities* and "White Angels" in *New England Review*. We wish to thank the editors of these publications for permission to reprint these stories here.

Out Far, In Deep has been published with the aid of grants from the following organizations: The Jerome Foundation, The First Bank System Foundation, The Arts Development Fund of the United Arts Council (with partial support from The McKnight Foundation), and The National Endowment for the Arts (with funds appropriated by the Congress of the United States). We also wish to thank the Minnesota Non-Profits Assistance Fund (supported by the Minneapolis Foundation) for its timely and generous support.

New Rivers Press books are distributed by

The Talman Company
150-5th Avenue
New York, NY
10011

Out Far, In Deep has been manufactured in the United States of America for New Rivers Press (C. W. Truesdale, editor/publisher), 420 North 5th St./Suite 910, Minneapolis, MN 55401 in a first edition of 1,200 copies.

for Carol and Matthew

CONTENTS

WHITE ANGELS

Everything went wrong that Saturday in November when Boggs rode up. I was minding my own business, loafing on the barnyard's split-rail fence. I watched the ducks and geese forage in slow circles in the front yard as father muttered curses and milked the cow. Milking is women's and boys' work. We had stone to draw, wood to chop and lug in, fence to mend. My mother should have been out here, squeezing and pulling, but her hands were crippled up with arthritis. My sisters used to do the milking, but they ran off to Manchester, left us high and dry. My brother died and went to his better reward (as the Reverend likes to call it) before he learned how to milk. That left me, Johnny-come-lately. I've done enough milking to fill a lake. But now the cow is scared of my pimples and won't let me near her.

"Hitch up the stoneboat, son. We'll draw a load before it gets dark." My father's bald head rested on the Holstein's black and white flank. The milk hissed into the pail.

Slow as cold molasses, I harnessed and hitched up the mare. When I got done, I went back to loafing. The old man pumped away between the cow's legs, and I daydreamed of Mercy Page.

Mercy Page steps out of the barn. The dark cloud that covers the sky is pierced by radiating spokes of sunlight. To soothe and dry my pimples, Mercy applies two plasters dipped in molasses and flour. Mercy's arms are veiled in soft golden hairs; her wrists are bare, her palms are white; her fingers are hot, like the cow's teats. After the plasters dry, she peels off the salves. "Thomas Granger, Junior," she says, soft as a hermit thrush, "your blemishes won't heal until you mend your ways."

"What?" I said.

"Who drove up?" my father asked.

"Drove up?"

"Somebody's come. Can't you see?"

I looked toward the front yard. The fattest man in Goshen had tethered his piebald cart horse to mother's hydrangea bush. "It's Sheriff Boggs."

Boggs lumbered toward us, a hand behind his back. The ducks and geese scattered as if the dog was loose.

"What's Ephraim want with us?"

"Come to help us draw stone," I said.

My father wanted to laugh (I could see it on his face), but he said, "Mind your manners, boy."

Puffing like a cow in labor, Boggs reached the fence where I was sitting. "Your pa around?"

"Nice day, Sheriff," said my father behind him.

Dull and slow, Boggs looked left, then right, out toward the field, back toward the house.

I pointed toward the stalls.

"There you are," he said. His fat hand clutched a pair of handcuffs. "You folks heard?"

"Whose cow got into Elijah's corn?" my father said.

"Kaiser gave up," said Boggs. "War's over."

Milk sizzled into the bucket. "We heard," my father said. Boggs snuck the cuffs into a pocket and studied the hard gray sky. "Cold north wind," he announced, as if he knew all about the weather. "Looks like snow."

"It'll rain, more than likely," said my father.

Scratching behind his right ear, Boggs gazed across the gathered stone in our new field. He appraised the distant dark conifers. "Think it'll rain, do you?" He jumped when the mare dragged the stoneboat into the muddy barnyard. He stared as if she were stolen. Something was gnawing at him. His stubbly chins quivered like a mass of frog eggs; his eyes squinted as if he were trying to look through a wall. Then he turned his nervous eyes on me.

2

He stared at my pimples, the talk of the town. At the Grange, the girls began to giggle when I came in. They'd whisper, "Watch out. Don't touch us." At church the Reverend Shoup forever sermonized about the sores, warts, eruptions, or blemishes upon the countenance of sinners. Our neighbor, Elijah Heath, believed the Reverend, heart and soul. Everywhere he went, he spread rumors: "That boy's sinned. Those pimples are a sign."

I glanced at Boggs. He wasn't staring at me anymore, and he wasn't listening to my father, who jawed about his rheumatism. Boggs gawked at our tom turkey.

The mare raised its tail and pissed a waterfall. The turkey flapped to a fence post right in front of Boggs. He yelled, "Get away from me!" and covered his face with his arms. He backed away. Then he slipped in the mud and went down like a steer hit between the eyes with a sledgehammer.

I fell off the fence laughing.

Boggs cursed a string of filthy words.

"What ails you, Sheriff?" said my father, hauling the milk pail out of the barn.

"That boy of yours is under arrest." Boggs flailed in the mud.

"Under arrest? What in hell for?"

"Buggery." He spat out the word as if it were dirt.

I figured it had to do with my pimples. "I can't help it if I've got sores."

Boggs shaved mud off his pants with the side of his hand. "You're going to jail, boy."

"No he's not," said my father. "I need him here. There's wood to chop and get in before winter comes."

"Come here, Granger." Boggs fished his cuffs out of the muck.

I hopped the fence, ran across the field, slipped into the woods. I hid behind a tree and listened for Boggs. If he had apoplexy chasing me, Elijah Heath'd be the first to blame me. I doubled back to the edge of the dark field. Boggs, like the Reverend in front of his sinning congregation, was waving his hand in my father's face.

To play it safe, I decided to sleep in the woods. I knew the woods. They were mine. I could name the flowers and birds, thanks to my sisters, and find the secret glade where the deer go down to die. I knew there was nothing to fear. Mountain lion and wolves had been hunted

3

out long before I was born, and bear were scarce as ice in July. My father had seen one bear in 60 years.

I wandered back into my grandfather's abandoned orchard. Sapsuckers had riddled his apple trees; there were more holes than bark. A few dwarf apples hung from their stems like shrunken heads in a wigwam. Dead limbs, broken by last year's heavy snow, lay on the ground. Bracket fungus grew on the rotting wood, white smiles in the gloom. In the summer, fairy rings sprang up in the grassy spot, and white angels opened their deadly caps near the pines. I crossed the stream that ran down from the mountain. Slivers of ice clung to the dark rocks like Christmas tree ornaments.

I wasn't afraid until the sky became black as the inside of a tomb. Then I started hearing noises—leaves crackling, the scurry of feet. Mice, I told myself. Maybe a squirrel, a deer? Something cracked a twig. Something thudded through the underbrush. Bobcat? Bear? A buck snorting sounded like thunder. Then I remembered the Indian stories I had read. I couldn't get them out of my mind. The Indians tortured a man by broiling his head over a hot fire. They stuck burning splinters into a soldier; he smoldered for days.

I thought about Boggs. Boggs wouldn't sit on that fence all night waiting for me. He'd go home for supper and for Sunday church service, and for Sunday dinner. Anybody as fat as Boggs had to eat all the time.

I crept back through the woods, circled the field, and slipped into the barn. The sheep bleated once as I stole through the stalls and climbed the ladder that led to the haymow. I lay down in the rowen. People were just like hay. They started off full of juice, like me, and ended up hollow as straw, like Elijah Heath.

Mercy comes to the haymow dressed in a moon-white gown. She carries plasters spread with a poultice of milk, bread, volatile liniment, and laudanum. Later, when she peels away the cloths, my sores are reduced, the pain is numbed. At dawn, I can see in her face my cure. My skin is as smooth as the mare's nose. Overjoyed, I leap up and hit my head on a rafter. Now Mercy stands at the barn doors; warm morning light pours through her dress. I avert my eyes, but the golden curves of her calves flash on the inside of my eyelids.

The mare woke me as she clopped out of her stall. Though a feeble sun was rising, I knew it would rain because the air smelled damp. My stomach snorted. I peeked through a crack in the barn boards.

Boggs' horse and cart were gone. I slipped down into the stalls. My father wasn't milking the cow. As I walked into the front yard, the ducks and geese squabbled and trampled each other to get their grain.

I opened the front door. My parents were sitting at the table like two marble statues. I turned to run, but Boggs came charging from behind the door and tackled me. We rolled off the porch into the muck at the foot of the steps. "Got you, you squirmy little devil!" He clicked the handcuffs around our wrists. The geese hissed and flapped their wings at him, but he batted them away. "Think you're so smart, don't you?"

We got up, yoked together like a couple of lopsided oxen.

"Easy does it, Sheriff," said my father. My parents stood on the porch, shading their eyes from the milky sun. "We talked it over, boy. Sheriff says this is the best way to handle it."

"Best get it over and done," my mother said. "This'll prove Heath's a liar once and for all."

I knew old man Heath was behind the whole thing. "We'll manage best we can," my father said, then he whispered something in my mother's ear. It took awhile, but then her face flashed like heat lightning at dusk. Bent at the waist, a dried cornstalk, she shuffled into the house.

"Sheriff said no one's going to hurt you, son."

My bones ached because Boggs had trampled me, but I supposed my father was right. Having pimples wasn't a crime. I hadn't done anything wrong. Besides, if I was in jail, I wouldn't have to do chores. My father'd have to do them all himself. Served him right for turning me over to Boggs.

"Let's go, before it rains," said Boggs. He was probably scared mother would change her mind and fetch the shotgun. He didn't know she couldn't pull a trigger with her wrecked hands. Finally she came back outside carrying two loaves of bread. They were still hot from the oven. They felt alive.

My father, the geese, and the ducks followed us down the lane to Boggs' cart. The ground had thawed. His piebald was fetlock-deep in muck. We stowed the bread under the seat, then climbed up, a couple of odd-sized twins. Boggs handed me the reins and said to my father, "Trial'll be the first of the month. Best get yourself a lawyer soon, Thomas."

"Old man Heath blames me for everything that goes wrong," I said.

Boggs nodded his head, his eyes half-closed. He had probably spent the night listening to my parents moan about Heath, and they didn't know the half of it.

"What's he blaming me for this time?" I asked.

No one answered. My father paced beside us, muttering to himself. I figured it had something to do with Heath's dead pig.

"Buggery," said Boggs. "And if he can prove it, they'll hang you."

I dropped the reins. "Hang me?"

"Heath can't prove a thing like that!" said my father. Boggs shrugged his bullock shoulders and picked up the reins.

"It's all because of my pimples, isn't it?"

"No," my father said.

"It's . . ." "I'm a day late already," said Boggs.

"Heath's just jealous of us, always has been," my father said.

"Best get yourself that lawyer." Boggs whacked his horse's rump.

"I'll speak to Blount," said my father as we pulled away.

The piebald trotted through a tunnel of whip-like saplings. At the edge of our property, the saplings gave way to deep forest. The cart wheels cracked on the rocks in the lane. "What's buggery, Sheriff?"

Boggs wiped his muddy hands. "You ought to know, you've done it with enough animals."

The boys at the Grange used to talk about that, but they didn't use fancy names. And they were lucky, they didn't have pimples all over their bodies or Elijah Heath for a neighbor. "Why does Heath always pick on me?" I asked.

"Heath pick on you?" Boggs' hill of a stomach shook up and down.

"I wouldn't laugh," I said, spying the low spot ahead.

Boggs kept on laughing until his horse pulled us straight into the muck, miring the cart to the axles.

Damn my luck, Boggs wasn't dumb enough to let me drive while he pushed. We were a couple of sweethearts, had to do everything together, had to push the cart halfway to town.

It was drizzling by the time we reached Goshen. The stores were locked tighter than the caps on acorns. The horse hauled us over the slick cobblestones toward jail. Up the street, church had let out. Reverend Shoup stood on the topmost step, his arms folded in front of him, his head bowed as his flock poured down the steps and scattered up and down Main Street, trying to save their sunday best from the rain. No one noticed me but Elijah Heath.

Heath scrambled down the steps. He scuttled across the street to intercept us. He grabbed the piebald's halter. Heath's face looked like a jack-o'-lantern. "Whoa!" he shouted.

"Let go, Elijah."

Stragglers from the congregation stopped to stare at us—mud-caked demons from one of Shoup's sermons on hell. "Gather round folks. Cast your eye on the devil's scum!" Heath's voice sounded like two rocks grinding together.

"Back off," said Boggs.

"Took you two days to bring in a boy," Heath said.

"Ride home before your supper gets cold," said Boggs.

Heath glared as if he could burn a hole through me. If he'd been carrying a gun instead of a Bible, I'd be dead now. He coughed up something disgusting and spat it at me. Then he dropped the halter.

Boggs whacked the horse's rump. We drove straight to jail, a low-slung building attached like a wart to Goshen's four-story, red brick town hall and offices. The jail was divided into a cell with a cot, window, and flush toilet (we had a privy in the shed at home), and an office with a desk and easy chair.

The minute Boggs went home for Sunday dinner, I began searching for a way out. I broke open my mother's loaf of bread—Boggs had kept one for himself—but a hacksaw blade wasn't hidden inside. I stamped the floor listening for a loose board. (Wasn't that how the king in *The Prisoner of Zenda* escaped?) I shook the cell door, I rattled the bars. I looked for but couldn't find a peg where Boggs kept his keys. I stood on a chair to inspect the bars on the window above my cot. The alley between the jail and the town hall glistened with rain.

"Thomas Granger, Junior."

It was Reverend Shoup, dressed in black and looking earnest.

"Dreaming of home, my boy?"

"Oh yes," I said, climbing down off my cot.

Shoup pulled up a chair and wove his fingers together. We talked about God's infinite wisdom, how all things followed his plan. I asked him what the plan was for me, and he said God worked in mystery. He said I should be mindful of my burden (he didn't mention my pimples) and of Elijah Heath's burden. When I asked him about Heath's burden, he reminded me that Heath's wife had died in childbirth. Then he asked me to join him in prayer.

Two days later, my father's voice woke me up. He couldn't believe I was still in bed at seven in the morning. I told him how Boggs' cart got stuck at the low spot, how we had to walk to town, how Boggs was scared of every noise in the woods. My father said that Lawyer Blount would be coming by in a few days. He warned me not to act smart; I needed Blount on my side. My father had something else to say but forgot it when I told him that Boggs had kept one of mother's loaves for himself.

Hearing that, Boggs decided to go out for coffee.

I put my chair on my cot and climbed up. I wriggled the loose bar out of the window frame. I handed the bar to my father, proud as a blue-ribbon winner at the fair. "I'm skinny enough to slip through that space. Then all I have to do is shimmy up the alley between the buildings."

My father thrust the bar at me as if it were a stick of dynamite. "You put that back where you found it, boy."

"Don't worry, I will."

"I don't want to hear talk about escaping."

"But Pa, they're going to hang me. Boggs said so."

"Boggs is all fat and mouth."

"I'm not taking any chances."

"Now listen here. You run off, it means you're guilty."

"What do I care? I'll go straight to Manchester."

"That's the first place they'll look. A boy green as you sticks out like a cow in the strawberry patch. No, you're staying put. We'll prove Heath a liar once and for all." He pulled his hat off and worked it between his hands. "Boy, I need you at home. Running that farm alone'll kill me. And if I go, your mother goes straight to the Poor Farm."

Boggs came back with his coffee. I was sitting on my chair, the bar clasped in my hands. I slipped it behind my back, but Boggs knew something was up. We were both stiff and silent as snowmen. Boggs shook the cell door to make sure it was locked. He looked us over as if we were prize cows at the auction.

I had to say something to get him off the scent. "Pa, I forgot to tell you about the dream I had last night."

"What?"

"The dream I had. I dreamt a white angel gave me a potion that cured my blemishes."

"White angel? Son . . ."

"Mercy Page, Pa. You know."

Boggs snorted like a surprised pig. "She wouldn't give you a second look," he said, walking back to his desk.

My father looked at me. "Now son, don't do anything foolish."

"Too late for that," said Boggs, leaning back in his chair. The springs shrieked. "He's already the first boy ever accused of buggery in the entire state of Vermont. Probably get himself hung for it. Serve him right."

"Shut up, Boggs!" My father turned back to me and squinted hard. "Just tell me one thing, Thomas..."

I stared back, solemn as the Reverend. "I never done anything."

My father seemed relieved.

"Don't matter, they'll hang him for his pimples."

"Boggs!" my father shouted. "If it comes to that..." My father flashed his eyes up to the window above my cot. He was right. If it came to that, then I'd escape.

Mercy comes to me with a canning jar full of leeches. She applies the leeches to my face and neck to draw and cleanse my blood. I grow limp and pale. I turn white as a mushroom. I'm too weak now to reach up and pull a leech off my face. Mercy weeps as she peels away the leeches like dark smooth scabs. She leaves me, her head down, tears in her eyes because she can't cure me. Her shoes clatter like the mare's hooves on the threshing floor.

I woke up with an aching bladder. But I couldn't go to the bathroom because Lawyer Blount was there, wiping his fogged-up glasses and pacing in his shiny black shoes. Enormous flakes of snow melted on his coat. "You're bleeding," he said, pointing to a red stain on my pillow. I covered myself with my blanket. "You understand the trial's just one week away? We'd better get our stories straight right now, Thomas Granger." He brought his face close to mine. "Did you do it?"

"Do what?" I tightened the blanket around me, but still shivered with cold. Boggs, off gobbling down breakfast, hadn't lit the fire yet.

"What Heath says you did—buggery."

"No."

"No, sir. You've got to no-sir and yes-sir me in that courtroom, boy."

"Yes, sir."

"Why are you shivering? Are you afraid?"

"I'm cold."

Blount pulled his glasses down his nose. "What about the sheep?"

"Never, sir. The animals are afraid of me."

"They're afraid of you because of what you've done."

"No, sir, because of my pimples."

"You buggered the cow, that's why she won't let you milk her."

"The cow's huge, sir."

Blount pushed his glasses back up his nose. "So you've thought about it. Then you did it when it was a calf."

"I was five years old then, sir."

"Heath's got a list long as your leg. He says he's seen you dozens of times."

I wanted to remind him that Heath hated me, had hated the grass under my feet from birth. And I hated Heath—right up to here. "Why would I do things like that in front of Elijah Heath?"

Blount blinked. He removed his glasses, polished them furiously with a snot-colored hankie. "You can admit you're guilty and ask for leniency. You can say you're a miserable sinner. They might give you a light sentence. You can plead not guilty. Heath would then have to prove his case, which wouldn't be easy. But if they find you guilty, you could hang."

"Heath's a liar," I said. "I want everyone to know it."

"Not guilty it is then," Blount said, looking at his watch. "We'll work out the details over the next few days." He glanced around for Boggs, who was taking up two bar stools at the counter at the restaurant. I couldn't hold it in another minute. I ran to the toilet and started to piss.

Blount opened the cell door and walked into Boggs' office. He closed the cell door. "Don't do anything stupid, Thomas. Boggs will be back any minute."

I pissed and pissed, a waterfall of piss that wouldn't stop. I was sure Boggs would come back before I finished. Just my luck. When I finally ran dry, I stepped into his office. I peeked through the keyhole at the fluffy snow falling on Main Street. The front door was unlocked. I knew it was a test. If I were guilty, I'd try to run off, like my father said. Maybe Boggs was waiting on the other side. Or Heath, with his gun. I went back to my cell, threw the cell door open, and sat down on my cot. I read a book. Boggs would tell everyone I was as innocent as a spring lamb. Heath would hate me hotter than a hickory fire.

Boggs didn't exactly dote on me, but he gave me more food and kept the jail warmer. On the morning of the trial, he brought me a wash bowl and a change of clothes. The clothes I had been wearing could have taken the stand without me. I scraped the mud off my jacket and wiped it clean. Then I took my first ride in a car, a Model T. We drove over the snowy roads to Chelsea where the tall white courthouse cast a blue shadow across the Common. Chelsea swarmed with people; it was like the Fourth of July. Everyone was trying to catch a glimpse of me. The courtroom was as noisy as the Fairlee cattle auction. But when Boggs brought me in, the room became quiet as a church. We sat down beside Blount, who acted as if he didn't want to wrinkle his suit. Behind us sat Reverend Shoup, nodding confidently, and my mother, who put her deformed hand on my shoulder. Her red knuckles looked crushed. I smiled at my father, but he didn't look up. He methodically pulled his round hat brim through his hands. Mercy was there, near the back, but we pretended we didn't see each other.

Then I noticed the jury, ten men and two women, staring at me as if I could fly. They were farmers or townspeople, wearing their sunday best, stiff and starched, wishing they were some place else. We stood up. The Judge flapped in, waving his black robe, hammered his gavel, got down to work.

"Thomas Granger, Junior," said the court clerk, as if everybody were deaf. "You stand accused of buggery—"

Shouts and yells filled the courtroom. A flash exploded. That photographer was thrown out; others were warned. "How do you plead?"

"Not guilty, your honor," I said, crisp and clear.

The room became quiet. I could hear my heart racing inside my rib cage as I walked up to the Bible, swore to God I wouldn't tell a lie, and sat down in the dark wooden chair. Unbuttoning my jacket, I noticed Heath's dried spit; it looked like a medal without a ribbon. I wanted to tell the jury how it got there. I knew the jury wouldn't trust a man who spat on boys.

Blount asked me simple questions that proved I was a hard worker and a good son, that I did my best despite my affliction. I kept my head bowed, my eyes on my toes. When I did look up, I saw Heath, his eyes burning like twin kerosene lamps at night.

The prosecutor from Montpelier, a slick, smart type in a pin stripe suit, asked me if I played baseball. I told him I had too many chores to do and lived too far from town to play baseball. That was all he wanted to know.

Blount then called a slew of witnesses—Reverend Shoup, some of my early teachers, a few relatives, some folks from the Grange—to swear that I was a fine fellow who worked hard and hurt no one, despite my affliction. The prosecutor managed to get each person to say that he or she really didn't know me that well.

The next day, the prosecutor called Heath to the stand. He knew me, all right. He charged up like a bull let out to pasture in the spring. Swearing, the oath, he sat himself down in the chair. His feet barely touched the floor.

After the swearing in, and a few simple questions, the prosecutor said, "Will you please tell the court what you have seen, Mr. Heath?"

"Yes, sir, I will, sir. I saw Thomas Granger, Junior," he said, pointing his dried up finger at me, "commit fornication with a cow, a mare, and a goat." He took a deep breath. "With a sheep, and a calf. And, as I live and breathe, with a turkey, a tom turkey."

Everyone in the courtroom was whispering the word turkey. The Judge hammered his gavel. Reverend Shoup stood up and tried to quiet the crowd. My mother turned white. Another photographer was thrown out of the courtroom for snapping a picture. The reporters scratched away in their note pads like chickens at a busted feedbag.

When order was restored, Blount took over. "Could you tell the court, Mr. Heath, where you observed these acts of buggery? For instance, where did you see Thomas Granger fornicating with the cow?"

"The cow?" Heath asked, pretending to remember. "That was in the barn. I saw him in the barn."

"And the mare?"

"That was in the field."

"And what about the goat, Mr. Heath?"

I held my breath.

"I don't remember," said Heath.

"Do you remember seeing him this year or last?"

"This year," said Heath. "No doubt of that."

I nearly laughed out loud.

"Mr. Heath, do you work at Granger's farm?"

"Of course not. I've got my own farm to tend."

"Then why do you spend so much time at your neighbor's?"

Heath spluttered like a squashed toad. He raised a hand in defense, but then couldn't think of anything to say. I felt sorry for him. The prosecutor was angry. He demanded Blount's last statement be stricken from the record. A few people in the courtroom nodded, but most shook their heads. They could see how crazy Heath was. The jury sat back, quiet as cows after a milking. The Judge advised the jury to ignore Blount's last question and Heath's reply.

I was recalled to the stand. As I walked up to take my seat, I felt sure people were on my side. Nobody could believe Heath's lies now.

"Do you have a goat?" Blount asked me. Blount was a genius.

"No, we sold it two years ago, when I was fourteen."

Again the courtroom grew noisy and again the Judge had to hammer his gavel for silence. I tried not to laugh. My parents were nearly smiling. The Reverend stroked my mother's hand as if that could make it better.

"No more questions," said Blount.

Now the prosecutor walked over, smiling, friendly, a hand behind his back. The courtroom grew quiet as a mousetrap. "How long have you known Elijah Heath?"

"All my life," I said. "So far."

A few people chuckled.

"Do you like Mr. Heath?" The prosecutor's voice was as gooey as a strip of flypaper.

"He's our neighbor," I answered. "I don't dislike him."

"But you don't really care for him, do you?"

"I feel sorry for him," I said.

"Oh? Why's that?"

"Because he's all alone, because he never had any children. His wife died, you know."

"Do you also feel sorry for him because you've played a few pranks on him?"

I lowered my head. "I never meant any harm."

"Oh? You never meant harm? But you did snip off his pea blossoms, isn't that right?"

"They grew back, sir," I said. "For once we had peas ahead of him, that's all. Heath was always bragging up his early peas, as if he was better because his came up first."

Some people snickered.

"I suppose you didn't mean any harm when you poisoned his pig?"

Everybody in the courtroom stopped breathing at the same instant.

"I didn't poison his pig."

"But it was poisoned. I have the examiner's report right here." He waved some papers.

"So?"

"So, tell the jury about white angels, Thomas Granger."

The courtroom was buzzing. The Judge hammered until there was silence. My parents looked like gray statues.

I didn't want to tell him about Mercy. I didn't want to drag her into this. "They are poisonous mushrooms," I said.

"That's correct," said the prosecutor. "Your sisters taught you all about them, didn't they?"

I nodded my head, staring at my parents. Had they told him everything? They turned away.

"Didn't they?" the prosecutor asked.

"Yes, sir," I said.

"Isn't it an interesting coincidence that Elijah Heath's pig died of poisoning caused by an amanita mushroom—a white angel."

Blount jumped up and said I was not on trial for killing a pig.

"That's true," said the prosecutor, "nor is he on trial for tormenting his neighbor. While other boys were busy playing baseball, Thomas Granger, here, was busy playing nasty tricks. He knocked down stone walls, cut barbed wire fences, and put dead fish in Heath's cellar; he fouled his milk tank, sowed grass seed in his garden, stole his sweet corn, and put rotten apples in his bins. And that's only half the story."

"That's all immaterial," Blount said. "Heath blames the boy for everything that goes wrong. Many of the events you describe are the result of natural events."

"Pigs don't happen to eat poisonous mushrooms," said the prosecutor.

"That's irrelevant to this case," said Blount.

"I think not," the prosecutor said. "The boy's pimples, his cruelty, the poisoned pig, and his fantasies are all relevant to the charges."

"Get on with it," the Judge said.

"Thank you, your Honor," the prosecutor said. He started to pace, a syrupy smile on his face. He circled around me, friendly as a stepped-on snake. "You have a friend you call a White Angel, don't you?"

Blount said the prosecutor was leading the witness; he rephrased the question. It gave me enough time to think of an answer. The last thing I wanted was to get Mercy into this mess. She was too good to be mixed up in this. Too pure. What we had was special.

"No," I said, "I don't have any friends. I don't play baseball, remember?"

"That's right," the prosecutor said. "I forgot."

I had him. The courtroom was silent as a cat ready to spring on something hidden in the grass. The prosecutor tossed aside a pencil he'd been fidgeting with. "But your White Angel is someone special, isn't she?"

"I said I have no friends."

"Yes, but she does things no one else can do, doesn't she?" I stared at Boggs. After all I had done for him. The pig was looking at the ceiling.

"I don't know what you're talking about."

"She can cure you, Thomas, can't she?"

"Your Honor," Blount said. "This line of questioning. . ."

The Judge must have seen something on my face, because he let the prosecutor go on.

"She can cure your blemishes, can't she, Thomas?"

"Please," I said.

"Just tell us what she does, Thomas. It's not black magic, is it?"

"No, no. . ."

"Tell us, Thomas."

"Please, don't. . ."

"Well, if you won't tell us, perhaps she will," the prosecutor said. "You may step down." He turned to the clerk. "Please call Mercy Page to the stand."

The clerk called Mercy Page.

"No," I yelled.

"You may step down," the clerk said to me.

"You don't have to drag her into this," I shouted.

"Mercy Page," the court clerk announced.

"Leave her alone."

"Please step down. Mercy Page, come forward."

Mercy had risen. The courtroom turned its greedy eyes on her. Licking their pencils, the reporters scribbled furiously. Another photographer snapped a picture, then was removed from the room.

Mercy was a golden light, more beautiful than a dream and purer than May grass.

"Step down, please."

A guard was trying to lead me off the stand.

"She doesn't know anything," I said.

Blount waved at me to get down.

"Leave her out of this."

"Mercy Page," said the clerk.

"Step down," Blount yelled.

"No, I won't step down. I'm guilty. She has nothing do with this. She's innocent. I lied. I'm guilty. Guilty. I'm guilty."

My parents collapsed like new born calves. Blount shook his head. Mercy gave me a sad, quizzical smile.

After it was over, they posed me in front of the courthouse. Everyone got one long look. The photographers lined up like a firing squad, and the reporters asked a thousand questions, scribbling down everything I said. When they put me into the Model T, I started planning my escape from the Goshen jail. I could almost see Boggs' stupid expression when he came in and found me gone. He'd search all around, then spy the missing bar in the window. I spotted Heath, looking self-righteous and content. The instant our eyes met, the hate came back like an ember bursting into flame. Then they drove me straight to Manchester prison.

HEARTWOOD

My head throbs, my eyes pulse. Too much dope, too much TV, I tell myself. I collapse into bed. "Henry," I say, "what you need is a good night's sleep." What I get is a spring zephyr, a gentle breeze that sways the elm outside my window, all night long. The elm moans like a trapped animal, and one of its twigs taps against the house at random intervals. By morning's gray light, I discover that the twig looks like a witch's finger, quivering black and gnarled three feet beyond my reach. I take several deep breaths and fall back into bed. When the sun comes up, the wind dies down, and I finally doze off. But not for long. A car with straight pipes, driven by a kid who worships horsepower, shakes the house as it blasts down the road.

I stare at the ceiling. I get up. I have to hunt down my clothes. My pants are gathering dust balls under the bed; my shoes are hanging on the bedposts; my shirt is missing in action. I blame the lumber and the seeds in the home-grown grass.

It's 1974. Nixon is erasing tapes and saying "I am not a crook." The war finally ends, but we know nothing we did stopped it. I quit my job in Cambridge and moved to the country. I'm tired of compromises and lies and half-truths. I raise vegetables, chickens, sheep, goats; I eat whole grains, drink herb teas, get into Zen, the *I-Ching*, a little yoga.

Yoga will straighten out my head, I figure, but before I get a chance to do one Salute to the Sun, Ora Appleton, the farmer up the road, knocks on my door.

"I'm up here, I'll be right down."

"Still in bed?" he yells.

I can't find my shirt. I jerk on my shoes, no socks, clomp downstairs. Ora is standing at the front door, wearing his dirty green work clothes, puffing his two dollar pipe. He's sixty years old, six foot six; his shoulders, elbows, and knees jut out at odd angles like the bones of a cow. He stares me up and down through the glass in the door as I zip up my fly. I open the door to a cloud of blue smoke; I gag and cough dramatically, waving away the fumes.

"You're a sight, Henry," he says. "Full moon keep you up?" He grins, showing me his four solitary teeth.

When I tell him about the elm, the branch, and the wind, he says, "Get your chain saw, cut it down."

I like his straightforward, no nonsense approach. I'd spend a week deciding whether the esthetics of the house and surrounding land would be ruined if I chopped the tree down. I'd spend another week contemplating the effects on the ecosystems. "I thought the tree could be useful," I say.

"Elm's elm," he says. "Makes half-good firewood, but it's a devil to split."

"What about erosion?"

"That hill behind your house is all grass."

"So?"

"Long as it stays grass, it won't go nowhere."

"What about how it looks?"

"What?"

"The tree. How it looks."

"It looks dead as my telephone, Henry."

I wonder whether or not he's right.

"Mind if I use yours?"

"What?"

"Your telephone. Mine's dead."

"Oh, sure. Sure, help yourself."

I figure he's probably right about the tree. I motion him toward the living room. "Want a cup of coffee, Ora?"

Ora nods, but I don't know if it's for the phone or the coffee. I know he drinks coffee as if it were water, so I put on the pot. I pour myself some breakfast, then wander back into the living room. The old man's on his elbows and knees behind the couch, resting his head on my Tibetan prayer rug.

"I didn't know you did yoga," I say.

"I don't. I was tracking down the phone."

I glance at the side table where I usually keep the phone. There's a blank square surrounded by an army of dust.

"You always hide it under here?" He hauls the phone in from beneath the couch, his pipe puffing symmetrical clouds.

I don't know what to say, either about the phone or Ora's smoking. I've coughed noisily whenever he lights up, but Ora never gets the message. I suppose it's because he's smoked in this house for thirty years. In his mind, it's the old Perkins place, and always will be.

"And here's your shirt." He unwinds the shirt from the cord.

"Must have had one too many last night." I wink and grin.

Ora dials the number.

I feel like an eavesdropper and retreat to the kitchen. The teapot sits on the stove's left burner; the right burner glows fiercely. I move the kettle over, eat granola mixed with raisins and yogurt, contemplate the spring morning. I listen to the birds quarrel over fence posts and nesting sites. I overhear Ora telling Ralph that when he comes back, he should bring a hacksaw and a plastic bag. I wonder what they're up to. Ora paces, grinning. He pauses, then picks up my pot pipe off the couch. He examines the brass fittings, the stem, the bowl. I shovel in mouthfuls of granola. For a second, I consider telling him the truth: "That's a pot pipe, Ora. Occasionally I smoke marijuana to alter my consciousness." The word marijuana would send Ora to the phone to call the sheriff.

"Don't forget those plastic bags," Ora says. He says good-bye, then he says, "Say, Henry, what's this?"

"What's what?" I ask, swallowing unchewed nuts. "That? That's a pipe."

"A pipe?"

"A pipe, from Nepal," I say. "People in Nepal are poor, so they use tiny pipes to save tobacco."

"Is that right," says Ora. He looks at the pipe from every angle. "How long were you and Ralph in Nepal?"

"Two years."

He looks at my bowl of breakfast cereal. "That where you started your vegetables diet?"

"No, I started that after I left the Peace Corps and moved here. But this isn't vegetables, Ora, it's granola and yogurt."

"That what they eat in Nepal for breakfast—grangola and yougut?"

"Yup. You want a taste?" I hold out the bowl.

Ora tries not to gag. He backs away. "I'll run along."

"I thought you wanted some coffee?"

He shakes his head as he walks to the door. I follow him down the driveway toward his car. Halfway there, he stops to take a hard look at the elm. He puts one of his long bony arms around my shoulder. "Looks like it's begun to lean."

"You think so?"

"Probably why it's making such a racket. You could cut it down easy."

"I don't know how, Ora."

He removes his arm from my shoulder. I know exactly what he'd like to say: "Only a goddamn fool doesn't know how to cut down a tree!" Instead, he shows me his solitary teeth again. "Didn't you cut down a poplar last year?"

"No, Ora. The wind blew it down. I just cut it up."

He jams his moist pipe stem into my biceps and hoots. "And then you tried to burn it!" Shaking his head, he cackles all the way to his car, crams himself into the seat. "Might be half a cord of wood there." His long legs stick up behind the wheel. "You coming with me?"

I stand in front of his Beetle not sure what to do. "I guess not. Thanks anyway."

"Gonna chop it down with an ax?"

"No."

"Better come with me then."

"Why, Ora?"

"'Cause I got your chain saw, remember?"

Ora's grin is filled with tobacco juice. He opens the door for me and I climb in. It doesn't occur to me that he might be setting me up for a trick, like the one he played last year with the poplar. I had asked him if it was good wood and he had said, "Sure, it's good. Cut it up, stick it in your stove, it'll be there in the morning." Must be a slow, hot burner, like oak, I thought. I cut it up, hauled it into my shed. That night I stuck the poplar in my stove. The next morning it was hissing, foaming, and giving off as much heat as a wet towel.

"I fixed your saw," Ora says as he drives up the hill toward his farm. "Loose connection in the ignition switch."

I thank him. He looks away as if I said the wrong thing. I notice

I'm shallow breathing and take several Cleansing Breaths. My head clears. I begin thinking Ora's right. Why make such a fuss over a dead tree? Ora's an expert; he's spent years working in the woods. To cut off that one limb, I'd have to borrow a ladder from Ora; I'd have to sharpen my ax or buy a blade for my bow saw. Then I'd have to return the ladder. If I cut the tree down, I'd learn how to do it and get some firewood in the bargain.

"Woodchuck!" Ora yells, pointing up the road.

I start talking about how wonderful it is to live in an area rich in natural fauna.

Ora accelerates. "Never had one in your garden?"

"No. Are they bad?"

"Worse. After we lost our dog, the woodchucks moved right in. Elmira didn't have much to can that year, and we didn't eat vegetables till we turned up the turnips come spring."

"Why didn't you just buy vegetables at the supermarket?"

Ora aims the car at the woodchuck, humping along at the side of the road. Ora catches up and slows down. He honks. The frightened animal breaks across the road. Ora crushes it with his right front tire. On its side, part of the woodchuck churns the dirt.

I don't know whether Ora's reason for killing wild animals is a matter of self-preservation or habit. He's shot and trapped everything that moves through the forests and meadows since he was six. When I consulted the *I-Ching*, wondering how I should handle our relationship, the book said "Fellowship with men in the open brings success."

We stop in front of his garage. Ora turns to me and says, "You'll need a good day to split that elm."

"What's a good day?" I study his eyes and lips to make sure he's not up to some new trick.

Ora turns away to climb out. When I open my door, Ora's English sheep dog comes over, pisses on the tire, then starts nipping at my cuffs.

"At twenty below, that elm'll split—" Ora snaps his thick fingers. The dog bounds for its lair beneath the hydrangeas. Ora opens the door to the breezeway that connects his house, shed, and garage.

"I can't stay long, Ora."

"You city folks, always rushing off somewhere." Inside, he shouts, "Elmira, we got company!" He ushers me into his warm kitchen where the odor of manure and bacon fills the still air. Ora slumps into a chair to unlace his heavy boots. He tells me there are four things to learn about chopping down trees. He tosses a boot into the corner. Four cats shoot out across the floor. "Put on the kettle, I'll draw you a picture."

While I fill the kettle with water, Ora shoves aside the breakfast plates and coffee cups, sweeps up the mounds of burnt tobacco, and wipes egg off the tablecloth with his sleeve. After a long search, he finds a pencil. For paper, he rips open an envelope and turns it inside out. Ora draws a tree trunk, draws a notch and a back cut on it. He explains how each cut is made and how each works.

"What else?" I say.

Ora pulls off his other boot and tosses it into the corner. "Don't be on the wrong side when the tree comes down."

"I get it. What else?"

"Where's that coffee?" Ora asks.

I forgot to turn on the burner. I light it; the gas hisses, then flames. Rolling up her sleeves, Elmira comes down from the upstairs bedrooms. She's short, dark, big shouldered, with silver-blue eyes that miss nothing. "Look what the cat brought in," she says. She knows I didn't sleep well last night and now she's wondering if I slept alone or with someone. She sets out three mugs and ladles in instant coffee and, before I can stop her, refined sugar. She folds her arms up and asks me about my surveying work. After I've told her what jobs I'm working on now, she asks if I'm going to keep at it or go to work in my father's factory. I tell her I'm staying here. They both shake their heads. "Why'd you want to stay here?" Ora asks. "Fella with your Harvard education."

I try to explain. The kettle starts to shriek. We talk about our gardens: who's going to have peas and early potatoes before July fourth. Talk about the garden reminds Elmira of the bright thing Ora did this morning.

Before she can say what it is, Ora interrupts, "Elmira, didn't you make some doughnuts? Aren't you gonna offer one to our guest?"

Elmira fetches two doughnuts out of the glass jar, sets them on a plate, and clanks the plate in front of me.

An hour later, Ora pulls on his boots and announces he's got to go out and cultivate the potato patch. I'm flashing on sugar and carbohydrates.

"Your saw's in the garage," Ora says.

"Thanks. I guess I'll be getting along."

"Stop by again," says Elmira.

"Thanks for the snacks."

"Don't mention it, Henry."

As I walk off, I notice the cats have woven themselves together under the wood stove. I walk through the breezeway into the shed. I roller-skate on the dog's food chunks scattered on the floor. I climb over the logs in the shed and enter the dark garage. Six yellow stripes of sunlight shoot through the cracks in the clapboards. Spotlit by knotholes, Ora's tractor looks like a cadaver worked over by medical students. The engine's gone, wires and hoses dangle disconnected, gas drips periodically from a glass filter. I pick up my chain saw and head for the garage doors. I run straight into the deer. The gutted carcass hangs by its hind legs from hooks in the rafters. A big mound of pink guts and clotted blood sits at my feet. The hide has been ripped down like a glove peeled back over itself, exposing the yellow flesh. I squat and do the Bellows Breath until I feel centered. I then walk toward the garage doors. They don't open. I panic. I kick and shove. Both doors fly open. I'm blinded by sunlight. Something tickles my neck and slides down my back. I run, screaming. Ora's dog howls and nips.

"Shot it this morning," Ora explains, trying not to laugh. "In the garden," he adds, his hand behind his back. Little jolts of laughter, like heat lightning, keep bursting from his mouth.

I glare at the dog, who keeps catching its snaggle tooth in my cuffs. I pick up my chain saw. I know it's legal to shoot a deer that's eating your vegetables, but I also know Ora. I thank him for fixing my saw.

Ora blows a megaphone of smoke across the yard. The barn swallows twitter on the line above our heads. With a guilty flourish that makes me flinch, he pulls a doughnut from behind his back. "We'll have you up for venison real soon." He puts the doughnut in my hand.

Deer steak! And me a vegetarian. I had to laugh. Ora belongs to a totally different species. How can I get angry at him? I can take a joke or two. There's no sense getting too yang about it, I tell myself. I laugh out loud imagining what I must have looked like shooting out of the garage as if a bull were on my heels. Ora's from a different culture. Ora's a natural man—rough, primitive, homespun. This is his kind of fun.

Would I have the nerve to play a prank like Ora's? As I walk down the dirt road, I try to dream one up. Nothing comes to mind. I observe the blue sky, the soft young leaves, the breeze full of flowery scents, the woodpecker hammering on a hollow tree. I cut across a field to avoid the stiffening woodchuck. I think of my friend Ralph, the philosopher and poet. Last fall, when we moved into the farmhouse, we took a walk and came across a dead deer, its white ribs smiles on the brown leaves. Two days later, Ralph wrote a poem that began, "O fallen star. . ." Now Ralph's in cahoots with Ora, bringing plastic bags and hacksaws to divvy up deer meat. A song sparrow sits on a fence post and sings its tireless song, "Maids, maids, maids, put on the kettle and get out the tea, tea, tea."

I march down the hill kicking stones, switching the chain saw from hand to hand until they both ache. Finally a prank pops into my head. I'll sic the sheriff on Ora and his dead deer. That'll get him stirred up. By the time I reach my porch steps, though, I lose my nerve. I decide to cut down the elm right now. If Ralph can eat deer, I can reduce an ecosystem to firewood.

I pop on my hard hat, pull down my eye goggles, slip on my gloves. I lower my ear mufflers. I step on the saw and pull the starter cord. Nothing. I check the gas, adjust the choke, yank the cord. Nothing. I crank the engine until my face turns red and my heart's thumping a hundred sixty beats a minute. Not a put-. Ora hasn't fixed the ignition, that was his pretext for getting me up to his house. What planning went into his practical joke! I storm into the house, shaking with rage. The house is full of blue smoke, as if Ora were still there, puffing his pipe nonstop. I run into the kitchen. The kettle on the stove is white hot, the room stinks of burnt rattan.

If Ora can do it, I tell myself, I can do it. I stuff a bandanna in my mouth and call the sheriff, Goshen's three hundred pound police force. When the sheriff finally comprehends what I'm saying, he tells me to call Weedler at Fish and Game.

Weedler asks for directions and hangs up. No hello, thank you, no good-bye. I'm hyperventilating and shaking hard from anger, nerves, processed sugar, instant coffee. I turn on the TV, but the cartoons make me feel worse. I wonder if I can turn off the carbo high with a pipeful of dope. I search for the pipe but can't find it. I'm sure Ora stole it for evidence. He's probably already called the Narc Squad. In Ora's book, poachers are American Robin Hoods; pot smokers are dope fiends. To play it safe, I fish the plastic bag of grass out of the flour canister. I take my cigarette papers, roller, and roach holder into the yard and bury them in the soft loam. I carefully wipe out the telltale trail of flour that runs back to the kitchen like a chain of eyeless daisies.

When I sit down, my pipe snaps in two in my back pocket. I close my eyes. I whisper my mantra until I feel centered. I fetch the chain saw to give it one last try. I flick on the ignition switch and pull the cord. The loose connection connects, the engine snaps into life like a mechanical alligator. I put on my safety equipment, then cut out the notch. It's as simple as Ora said. I move around to the other side of the tree, set my bar parallel to the ground, and lever the screaming chain into the trunk.

Ralph's face appears through a snowstorm of woodchips. "I'm almost done," I yell.

Ralph purses his lips, shakes his head, and waves a finger. I think he might know something I don't. I pull the whirling chain out of the cut. He waits for the saw to idle before he asks, "How come you're cutting it down?"

I tell him about the twig, the wind, the all-night session I've just had.

Ralph tugs back the hood of his sweatshirt. He pushes up his sleeves. "I thought you were a vegetarian?"

"I am." The chain saw splutters and dies.

"An elm is like broccoli, Henry. It feeds others, living or dead."

"I know all about that. What about a deer, Ralph?"

"That's different. Dead, a deer serves only one purpose—to feed the living."

"Then the important question is how the deer got dead."

Ralph pauses to reflect. "What deer are you talking about?"

"The one Ora shot this morning."

"Oh. That one. It's legal to shoot a deer if it's eating your garden."

"We both know Ora likes shooting anything that moves, anywhere."

"He is a breed apart," says Ralph. "What's eating you?"

"Me? Nothing. Heck no. It's just the first tree I've ever cut down."

"You should have left it alone, it wasn't hurting anyone."

"Neither was the deer."

"When in Rome . . ." he says. "Eat deer." He shows me his soft, white palms. "Hey, the important things don't change. Come on, I've got something for you."

I follow Ralph over to the hand-me-down Ford his parents gave him, eleven miles to the gallon. Ralph unlocks the cavernous trunk and waves his hand back and forth across the space.

I push back my goggles and lower my face into the darkness, into hundreds of bristling seedlings. "Don't tell me."

"You got it," says Ralph. "Give me a hand, will you?" He reaches in to haul out the huge tray.

"I don't want any dope, Ralph."

"You've given up smoking?"

"You've given up vegetables."

He thinks it over. "Give me a break, Henry. I can't haul this stuff up to Ora's. He probably thinks it's for sex maniacs. If anybody asks, just say they're tomato plants. I'll pick them up on my way back down."

We heft the seedlings into the kitchen. Ralph smells the incinerated rattan handle. I try to explain that it's not pot, but a nasty look stays on Ralph's face, even after he climbs into his car. The muffler's gone, the car explodes and roars pushing itself uphill. That was him this morning. He was at Ora's, shooting that deer.

I drag the tray from the kitchen table to the back room to the shed. At each spot, a sign saying HERE ARE THE POT PLANTS seems to light up when I put the tray down. I'm hauling the tray back into the kitchen when I hear a car skid to a stop outside. It's a white car with a government logo on the door. I stand there watching, the tray of pot seedlings behind me on the table. A man climbs out of the car and starts walking toward the house. I'm sure it's the Narc Squad. There's no way I can flush all those seedlings down the toilet in time. The guy walks up to the front door. He's wearing a raincoat; his face is as bland as the inside of a potato.

"Ora Appleton live here?" he asks through the glass.

"No, he's the next house on the left." I point up the road.

It's Weedler from Fish and Game. He looks at me through the front door, turns away, then turns back. "You the guy who called?"

"Called who?"

"You're the guy," he says. He walks down to his car. He guns the engine, sprays sand and stones. He means business, you can tell by the skid marks he leaves in the dirt. A plume of dust wafts into the air like a meteor's tail.

I run to the phone and dial Ora's number. He doesn't answer. For a moment I feel relieved. They're not there; they can't get busted. Then I remember Ora's phone is dead. I tell myself not to worry, the deer's legal. It's legal. It has to be legal. Ora's no fool.

I go outside. The elm is waiting for me. The notch gives me a toothless grin. I flick the ignition switch and pull the cord. The saw starts. I turn it off, I turn it on. For some reason it's working perfectly. Maybe

Ora fixed it after all. Maybe it wasn't a pretext. Maybe he didn't set me up for a prank. Maybe I ran into the deer by accident. I attack the elm. Woodchips fly, the tree groans, the heartwood begins to snap fiber by fiber. Sotto voce, I practice yelling timber. I check to make sure I won't be on the wrong side when the tree comes down. The tree settles down, the back cut clasps its wooden teeth on my bar. The chain whirls, tosses out a few more chips, then stops with a clunk.

I walk to the shed to fetch the ax, iron bar, and wedges. Weedler's car roars down the road, throttle wide open. I look hard to make sure Ora and Ralph aren't handcuffed in the back seat.

At the tree, I shove the wedges into the back cut; they slide in as easy as suppositories. I ram the bar in. I push down. Nothing happens. I can't even make the tree creak. Ora and Ralph drive up, get out. I wave them over.

"Am I glad to see you," I say.

Neither of them seems glad. They both stand like condemned men, hands pushed to the bottom of their pockets. They don't even laugh at my Moby Dick—the chain saw buried up to its handguard, dripping oil and gas. Ora glances up at the tree and says, "Should have told you about the lean."

"What lean?" I ask.

"The tree's leaning on your back cut."

"So?"

"You should have put the notch where the back cut is."

Ralph pushes down on the iron bar.

"Think you can lift ten tons with that toothpick?"

"Ora? Why didn't you tell me about this lean business before?"

"I did. I said the tree's leaning."

"But you didn't tell me to take it into account."

"I forgot." He blows smoke. I could swear he's grinning. "Let me use your phone, then I'll help you out."

I wave a hand toward the house as his calm and unruffled "forgot" wobbles through my head like a flat tire on dry pavement.

"Weedler caught us red-handed," Ralph whispers. His voice sounds as if someone were strangling him. I can see he's going to cry. "Weedler confiscated my car, Ora's gun, and the deer. He's going to throw the book at us—jail, fines, the fucking works."

After what Ora's done to me, I'm glad they're getting what they deserve. "You're kidding," I say.

"Do I look like I'm kidding?"

"Ora'll weasel his way out of it, Ralph."

"Not this time. You're supposed to leave the deer where you shot it; you're not supposed to gut it; you're supposed to call Fish and Game."

Already my indignation is wearing off. Whatever Ora's done to me, he doesn't deserve to go to jail, and he's got no money to pay a fine.

Ora's at the kitchen window, waving to us.

I remember the tray of seedlings. I race in, slamming doors, shaking the floor. Ora is sitting at the kitchen table, brushing his fingers through the seedlings. I clap him on the back. "Too bad about Weedler." I hover over him like a bee buzzing spring's first flower. "How about a cup of coffee, Ora?"

With shaking hands, I put the pan on the stove. Ralph stumbles in, his shoulders slumped. He crashes down into a chair. "What'd the lawyer say, Ora?"

"He said I shouldn't have shot the deer, shouldn't have gutted it, and should've called Fish and Game first thing."

Ralph is trying to gulp down the tears. Ora's being stoic. I feel like I'm made of broken egg shells, with all the fluids dripping out. They're sure to see it. I keep busy setting up the three cups of coffee. I pull out spoons and napkins. I line up the cups left to right. Ora takes milk and sugar, Ralph milk; I take it black. I realign coffee cups. I grab the instant coffee jar, ladle in heaping teaspoons. The pan on the stove refuses to boil. I eye Ralph, then eye the pot plants. I walk to the table. "Ralph, give me a hand." I grab the tray. "Ralph?"

Ora clamps his long fingers on the tray's rim. "Henry," he says, "there's something I want to know."

My hands tremble violently, my heartbeat shoots way up. I decide to deny everything, no matter what.

"Are you going to put some water in that saucepan?"

For an instant the room fills with gray space. I lower my head to stop myself from fainting. I fill the saucepan with water.

"Tomato plants," says Ralph to Ora, who's rubbing a seedling stem, sniffing his fingers.

"Tomato plants from Nepal," I add.

Ralph and I heft the tray to a dark corner.

Ora shakes his head. "Like that pipe of yours?" Ora asks. "Ralph, you got one of those little pipes from Nepal?"

"No, I don't smoke," Ralph says.

Ora sucks on his pipe. "Neither do you, Henry." He pokes me in the ribs. "Do it on the sly, don't you!"

"What are we going to do?" Ralph moans.

"Nothing we can do," says Ora.

The water begins to hiss. I ladle instant coffee nuggets into the three mugs, then remember that I've already done that, and ladle some of the coffee out. I try to figure out some way to get them out of the mess. Zip comes to mind. Ora drums the tabletop with his fingers.

"It could not be worse," Ralph whispers.

"Was the deer really in your garden?" I ask.

"On his way," says Ora.

"What bastard sicked Fish and Game on you," Ralph says.

The water in the pan fizzes, a lazy wisp of steam rises slowly into the air. Ora and Ralph are both staring at me. My heart is pumping itself out of my chest. "Hey, don't blame me just because I'm a vegetarian."

Ora jerks back his head and smacks the table. "I'd never think that. You're a friend." He stands up and looks at the saucepan. "To hell with coffee. Let's chop down that damn tree."

"Wait a minute," I say. "I've got it. You did try to call Weedler this morning. Your phone was dead, so you came down here. You told me you were calling him. You tried twice. It's not your fault he wasn't in."

They both stare at me. Ora grins. "Couldn't have done better if I thought of it myself."

A tentative, feverish smile appears on Ralph's face. "Will it work?"

"Sure it'll work," says Ora, "if Henry here sticks to his story."

"It'd be perjury," Ralph says.

"For friends?" I ask.

Ora slaps the table. "Let's chop that tree down, then celebrate. Tonight you fellas come up to my place. Elmira'll put on the feed. What do you say?" He clomps off toward the front door, Ralph at his side.

I turn the burner off and set the pan aside. I take a few deep breaths to calm myself. Fellowship with men in the open brings success.

Outside, Ora has attacked the elm with my ax. At each stroke, elm wedges fly, somersault, fall to earth. Ralph stands nearby, shifting from foot to foot. The heartwood snaps. Everybody yells timber at the same time. The tree groans, twists, then falls, quivering and crackling, sending a shower of broken twigs through the still air.

PROVIDE, PROVIDE

The temperature was 101 degrees on Winfield's unshaded Division Street. Motorcycles sank into the hot macadam, rolled over, oozed fluids like skid row drunks. Twelve hundred miles from home and an ocean breeze, I plodded through a half-dozen houses, looking for a year-long rental at a reasonable price. By the time I reached Priscilla Crett's house, the heat had impaired my judgment. A $50 saving on rent seemed like the bargain of the month, and her cool, stone house felt energy efficient. I should have been more observant. I should have checked behind the curtains, inspected the oil burner, added up the electricity, gas, and oil bills. I should have considered the circumstances: I was replacing Priscilla in St. Steven's English Department, and I was taking over her home. My public and private lives would both be under constant surveillance. I should have weighed the consequences. If Benjy, my brother's little genius, scribbled on the walls, or if my friend Gail left telltale stains on the mattress, the blemishes and blots would end up in my dossier. I should have realized that in an already depressed job market, I couldn't afford to take risks. Instead, I said, "No need to show me around, Ms. Crett, I'll take it."

She wrung her hands. The tendons stood out like guy wires. She smiled, unsure. Then the cat appeared, walking across the table, pausing to sniff the melted butter. "Do you like cats?" she asked.

"Love 'em," I said, petting. "She's a real cute blue Persian."

"Isaac is a he," Priscilla corrected. She picked him up and plunked him into my arms. Long blue hair, stiff whiskers, intense green eyes, Isaac examined me while Priscilla examined us. Taut as a mousetrap, she formed a church-and-steeple with her fingers. "Isaac can't accompany us to England because of the quarantine. I've considered taking my sabbatical elsewhere, but Eliot's late years..."

While Priscilla went over the details, I glanced around at the walls (yellowish, sedimentary fieldstone) and the furniture (pine or some other inexpensive wood). The house was supposed to look like a Frank Lloyd Wright.

"...This will be our first real separation."

My nose itched. "Does the rent include utilities?"

"No, it doesn't. Here are last year's bills. They're lower than usual. We had a mild winter."

"Mild? When I interviewed here last January, the temperature never got above twenty degrees."

"That's mild for Minnesota."

I sneezed and blew my nose, then pushed the bills aside.

"Let me show you Isaac's room," Priscilla said. She led me down a corridor. "Isaac eats Nine Lives Liver and Bacon Mix, exclusively. Half a can, twice a day. We switched from dry food. It causes cystitis."

Who's this "we?" I wondered, looking over Isaac's carpeted room: six yellow balls, four dead rubber mice, a bathtub of kitty litter, a disemboweled scratching post, a shelf of cat-care books, and a pyramid of cat-food cans. As Priscilla described Isaac's daily routine, I estimated how much it would cost to feed him. About 10 bucks a month, unless I mixed in cheaper chow. Still, the rent was reasonable compared to the rents of the other houses I had seen, and a steal compared to Boston, where Gail and I paid twice as much for half the room. I wasn't going to get Big City Culture (Winfield had one theater—the kind that shows last year's blockbusters for two weeks). But I was going to get handfuls of lithe, blue-eyed Scandinavian co-eds—the campus was filled with them—so I didn't expect to be bored.

"I'll take it," I said, blowing my nose.

"Summer cold?" Priscilla asked.

I nodded yes through my hankie.

The first thing Gail said was, "You jerk, you're allergic to cats."
Debarking passengers at Gate 25 in Logan Airport stared at the jerk.
"It's a great house," I said.
"Cheap, you mean."
"You'll see when you visit."
"Visit? Last week you were begging me to live with you."
"I don't think you'll want to live in Winfield, Gail."
"Especially if you don't want me to, Richard."
"Hey, I want you to visit so you'll know what to expect."
Between June and September, I said good-bye to Gail and Boston.
Gail would go off to work, and I'd walk down to La Vie de France
for fresh croissants and cafe au lait. Flakes of buttery pastry stained
my book on Frost's landscapes. As I arranged a sentence in my head,
a waitress invariably asked, "More coffee, sir?" In the afternoon, I'd
sip cappuccino and watch the world jog by from the tables of the Le
Bistro. Under an umbrella, I'd work fitfully, unable to build the usual
mountains out of molehills. To clear my head, I'd stroll along the
Charles, watch the seagulls bicker and wheel, the sculls skim by like
water bugs, the runners sweat beside the shore. Then, suddenly, it was
time to leave. We hugged and kissed. Gail said she'd visit soon. Under
a blue sky, the sun rising at my back, I drove off. Her image—her green
eyes, her brown hair, the peculiar way she curled her hand waving
good-bye—lingered all the way to Ohio.

Two days later I stood in front of my mailbox in the Thorsen Student Center at St. Steven College. Inside I saw a telegram, and the letter from Priscilla with the keys to her house. Nobody had told me the combination to my box. Sunday afternoon, the place was empty. I had no desire to spend another night in an expensive motel. Isaac would starve to death. TRAGIC NEWS. STOP. ISAAC DEAD UPON ARRIVAL. STOP. SORRY.
"Well, how do you like it?" A great bony hand clapped me on the back. It was Jensen, the medievalist—tall, fair, white as a bar of soap.
"Like what?"
"Winfield? St. Steven?"
"Oh. Wonderful. Couldn't be better. But no one left me the combination for my mailbox."
"Combination?" Jensen began searching for my box, whispering my

name. "Richard Cyp... Cyp... Here you are Rich." He snapped open the door with a flourish and removed my mail. Under the St. Steven's honor system, he explained, there was no need for combinations or locks on any doors. He eyed my telegram. "Hope it's nothing serious." He fetched his mail and strode away.

I tore open the letter from Priscilla. I put the enclosed house key on my chain. Six blonde, long-legged co-eds, wearing abbreviated cutoffs and tight T-shirts, their nipples pointing to heaven, marched to their boxes and popped open their doors with practiced ease. I opened the telegram. WELCOME TO MIDWEST. STOP. HOW'S SMALL-TOWN LIFE? STOP. CAN TAKE OFF SEPT 11 TO 20. STOP. VISIT THEN? STOP. MISS YOU. STOP. GAIL.

As I shoved the key into the front door lock, I heard Isaac meow mournfully inside. The poor cat was lonely, I thought. I put him in his room and closed his door while I moved my belongings into the house. Later, after I returned the U-Haul, I gave Isaac some food. He refused to eat. He curled up his nose at the milk I offered. I petted him, scratched under his chin, rolled his balls at him, talked baby talk. He shied away. My nose itched whenever I touched him. I thought he'd get used to me soon enough.

I settled in. The house contained more studies and bedrooms than I remembered. I couldn't understand why Priscilla, a spinster, needed two studies. I figured the fewer rooms I'd have to heat the better. I closed off all the superfluous rooms. That left a bedroom/study, the living room/dining room, Isaac's room, the bath, and the kitchen. I hauled out my typewriter and my book. I set aside the first three chapters and sat down at the desk in front of Chapter Four, covered with buttery stains and scribbles. Isaac tried to add a few marks of his own. I put him out. He howled and scratched at the door while I jotted a note to Gail: "Dear, Sept. 11-20 is the worst possible time for a visit. Classes are just getting under way. You know how frantic I get. Things should settle down by October 7. See you then?" My nose dripped like a slow leak in a faucet; my eyes itched.

School orientation took an entire week. I stole away as often as possible and wrote my lectures in my office at the library. But the great stone building—no doubt designed by the same amateur who designed Priscilla's house—closed each evening at Vespers. I had to work on my book at home. Ten pounds of unappeaseable meows waited for me behind the front door.

On the first day of classes, I found Isaac sitting like a sphinx on the radiator. I had a feeling something was up. I petted him. The radiator was hot. I turned the thermostat down to 62. The next day I found him squatting in his kitty litter, straining like a soldier at inspection.

A week later, I was struggling to keep afloat in a sea of freshman themes and class preparations. Yet Isaac was on everyone's mind. Ms. Thayer, one of my colleagues, stopped me in the hallway. "How's Isaac?"

"Isaac," I said, "is adjusting poorly to Priscilla's absence."

"Better take care of him," she said. "He's Priscilla's only child."

I had a sudden sinking feeling as I realized that both my teaching and my pet-nurturing skills would be on display all year long. I experienced a similar feeling the following day when I discovered that the living room drapes covered a thirty-foot expanse of drafty windows. Through the cold glass I saw, out in the yard, cleverly hidden by foliage, the air conditioner I had overlooked in June.

"He's very finicky," Ms. Thayer said. "And often ill."

"He spends a lot of time in his pan."

"Better take him to the vet, just to make sure."

"I suppose I should," I said, wondering when in hell I'd have the time.

"I don't envy you," she said. "With three new classes to prepare, 75 themes a week to grade, and a book to write, you probably don't have time to..."

"See a movie?"

"Fart," she whispered.

"I've seen 'Pinocchio' at the Majestic four times already."

"Really?"

"Would I lie?"

"How's Gail?" she asked.

"OK," I said. A bell rang in the slick, waxed hall. Co-eds in jeans so tight they made me squeak danced from one class to the next.

"You'll feel more at home once she's here," she said.

What else did she know? Did she know that I was tired of making love cinque contre un, that one of my sexiest students seemed willing to do most anything for an "A"? I knew that Ms. Thayer, untenured and nervous, was married. She had applied for a Fulbright. If she got it, I'd replace her—if the Department liked me.

To keep the Department from disliking me, I called the vet. Priscilla's card arrived the next day: "Dear Richard, How's Isaac getting along?" I should have written back, "Dear Pris, Although the radiator has four legs and Isaac rides it every day, he is not getting along." Instead, I abandoned reams of essays on "My First College Experience—Expectation Filled or Failed?" and drove 25 miles south to the vet in New Plat. I could see Isaac's dander floating through my car. I sneezed until my sides ached.

The best cat doctor in Rice County, Dr. Morris Flexnor, hoisted Isaac onto his stainless steel examining table. He poked a thermometer into Isaac's rectum, prodded his abdomen, and pried open his jaws. I blew my nose a half-dozen times.

"Cold?" said Dr. Flexnor, his voice smooth as fine brandy.

"I don't think so. He strains in his kitty pan."

"I meant you."

"I'm allergic."

"You adore cats, don't you?" Flexnor said.

I didn't want to disillusion him.

"It seems that Isaac's urethra is blocked. A common condition in male cats."

"I have writer's block," I said. "Do you suppose Isaac caught it from me?"

Flexnor assured me that cats don't catch human diseases and went on to say that Isaac's problem could probably be cured without resorting to surgery. He begged me to stop poisoning my cat with dry foods containing high ash contents.

A dead Isaac is all I need, I thought, as Flexnor, patting me on the back, led me to a waiting room filled with anxious patients.

"Isaac will have to remain here for several days for flushing and tests. That should clear things up," said Flexnor, ever kind and gentle. "Though he may relapse, at any time."

The room glowed with sympathetic faces. Flexnor squeezed my arm meaningfully. Shit, I thought, I have to come back.

I decided to make some basic changes: Isaac had to be pampered.

I had to stop sneezing. I had to devote more time to class preparations, and I had to get out from under an avalanche of unmarked essays. I wrote Gail, told her about the albatross I was forced to bear and begged her to be patient with me. I went to the allergist for tests and had a prescription filled. Returning unmarked essays, I told my students they were going to learn to self-evaluate. Over lunch, in Thorsen, Christine Christensen told me what a marvelous idea self-evaluation was. I corrected her syntax and dreamt of other marvels we could work on together.

Isaac has to be pampered, I told myself, ignoring the hiss of sleet across my windshield as I drove to New Plat to pick him up. He must be pampered, I reminded myself as he pissed all over the back seat of my car on the way home.

I gave him the run of the house, petted him twice a day at least, fed him unadulterated Nine Lives. When I received the bills from the vet, allergist, and pharmacist, I realized that pampering didn't come cheap. But I stuck to it. By November I saw results. Isaac was happy and my nose was happy. I had caught up on my essays, had prepared a few classes in advance, and had forgotten about Christine C and her "A."

I needed a mature woman. I called Gail and asked her to spend Thanksgiving plus the last week of November with me. She said she had to check her schedule at work. She asked about my work. I told her my chapter was in limbo—I couldn't think about Frost in the middle of the prairie—but I was scoring points with my colleagues by throwing potluck B.Y.O.B. dinner parties.

Nothing gold can stay. On Veterans Day the temperature swooped to 10 degrees, an abusive wind began to blow, and Nine Lives changed its Liver and Bacon Mix to Hearty Liver Chunks. The price went up 12 cents a can. Isaac buried the chunks deep in the rug. I should have warned Priscilla: "Dearest Pris, At wit's end, etc., etc....Nine Lives etc., etc....Isaac will eat only dry chow; Flexnor advises against, etc...."

After paying $239 to fill the oil tank ("P.S.: Your house is as porous as kitty litter."), I took action against the weather by insulating the house. Despite my efforts, the furnace rattled and groaned, pumping hot water to the radiators in a vain attempt to satisfy the thermostat. The red marker in the oil tank gauge sank to the bottom like the

Pequod. I moved my bed, desk, and books into the living room, closed off my bedroom/study, and turned the thermostat down to 55. Now the furnace seemed less prone to apoplexy. My checkbook took a breather.

"Mr. Cyp, this is Christine. I'm very upset over my latest grade. Could we discuss it?"

What could I say? Besides, it was almost Thanksgiving, and Gail hadn't written or called. "Why don't you come over."

"Really?" she asked, all delicate innocence.

I scarcely had time to straighten the bed before she arrived, breathless, her chest heaving. To calm the turmoil, I offered her some wine.

"Mr. Cyp," she said, "it's against school policy."

The little gamine, I thought, as I walked into the kitchen to fetch the bottle. Working the corkscrew, I watched Christine settle down, discreetly, on my bed. If she hadn't come to seduce me, why were her drink-to-me-only eyes lined with lashes as long as Isaac's whiskers? Why were her jeans as tight as olive skins? Why did her blouse remind me of Salome's last veil? Lucky Isaac hopped into her lap and rubbed her everywhere while I struggled with the engorged cork. Moments later, I handed her a glass. I looked down her blouse as I poured the wine. No bra. We discussed her mark. But nothing she said proved she deserved a higher one. We fell silent. Isaac departed her lap for the kitty pan. Christine set aside her glass. Now was the time for her to stare deeply into my eyes, to unbutton her blouse, to peel the delicate fabric back over her soft shoulders. The phone rang. I let it ring. Christine finally picked up the receiver and handed it to me.

"Hi. It's me. I'm sorry I couldn't call sooner. Work's been hell. The Christmas rush began early. I've got good news, though. I can come out December 17th and stay until January 3rd. How's that sound?"

"Sounds great, I'll call you back."

"Why can't you talk?"

"I'm conducting a class."

"A private tutorial, I suppose."

"Come on," I said.

Gail apologized, said she'd call back to let me know the details. I said good-bye and handed Christine her glass. "Sorry, where were we?"

"Mr. Cyp, it's against school policy," said my little angel, setting her glass aside. She reached into her back pocket. I don't know how she got her hand in there or how she managed to pull her blue book out. "Read my exam again, will you? It deserves more than a 'B' minus."

I took the paper. Dutifully I began to read. When I looked up, she was gone. I ran to the front door. Fresh tracks filled with glittery snow went off in every direction. I closed the door and turned around to find Isaac squatting in his pan, straining like Sisyphus near the summit. "Piss, damn you!"

After conferring with Dr. Flexnor, I called England and explained to Priscilla that a urethrascopy is an operation recommended for male cats suffering from recurrent cystitis.

"I understand," she said. "Proceed, proceed, by all means."

"You also understand the operation will cost $150, plus Flexnor's unpaid bill for $78, and this phone call?"

"I'll send you a check first thing in the morning," she said.

"Listen," I said. "How about a new cat—cheap."

Long, costly silence.

I drove the cat down to the vet again. Saturday, I called Gail. I told her I couldn't wait for her to come out. She said my professorial voice had sounded funny.

Ten days passed by without a word from Flexnor. Had Isaac run out of lives? No such luck. A nurse called to say that the operation had been a complete success. Her voice was bright and charming despite the snowstorm. I glanced at my moribund chapter, which was showing the faintest blush of life. I glanced out the window at the storm that had brought out travelers' advisories. I asked if I could drive down the following day. The nurse said I could, but I would have to pay for boarding.

Flexnor's love for *Felis domesticus* did not extend to *Homo sapiens*. I flung on my parka, rammed my appendages into gloves and boots, kicked ice off the garage door, started the car, and crawled to New Plat in weather as turgid as my recent prose. Poor Isaac. Flexnor had shaved his tail and hind legs, and encased his head in a megaphone-shaped piece of plastic. "You may experience some incontinency."

Thank God it's not my house, I thought.

But then, in a tableaux vivant, I saw Priscilla sitting down to write my recommendation. She sniffs the air, curls her nose. The acrid odor of cat urine infuses her remarks. "Am I supposed to follow the cat around with a kitty pan?"

"If you have the time, of course, that probably would prevent most accidents. We usually suggest a few extra pans, placed strategically. On the plus side, Isaac can now return to dry food. His urethra is substantially enlarged. Unfortunately, we ran into some unforeseen complications, so the bill is higher than anticipated."

"That's great. How am I supposed to explain that to his owner. She's in England."

"He's not yours?"

"I wouldn't spend good money on a cat, Dr. Flexnor. Isaac belongs to Priscilla Crett."

"But of course, the Cretts."

"Cretts?" I said.

"Priscilla and Bart," said Flexnor, petting Isaac. "In that case, I'll split the difference." He tallied figures, divided by two, and came up with $273. "I'll need a check before I can release the cat."

Flexnor insisted on cash-and-carry though he knew the Cretts, knew they would pay, knew it would strap me, after I explained my finances.

"Don't you have a carrying case?" he said, as I slogged off into the drifts.

My car was the carrying case. Isaac squatted, pissed. Bart Crett, I thought. Who would have imagined? I switched on the radio. Travelers' advisories had become warnings. I drove with extreme caution, happy that my pet-nurturing days were over—Isaac was cured—and my most difficult semester was grinding to a conclusion, and my relationship with Gail was becoming more permanent. Halfway home, a semitrailer loaded with Christmas turkeys, hellbent for the South Side stockyards, forced me into a ditch. "Shit!" I shouted. Isaac needed no prompting.

"Pederson," said my chairman in his clipped Navy manner.

"Jorg, this is Richard Cyp. I guess despite the storm school is open?"

"Rich, St. Steven closed only once in 95 years."

"That must have been during the blizzard of '76."

"No, when the central heating plant blew up."

"Was that it '76?" "No, we were open then."

"I get it. Look, Jorg, I've got a problem."

"My boy, if you can't drive, walk. Do you wonders."

"It's not that. I'm stranded in New Plat, Jorg."

"Is it some girl, Rich?"

I told him about the cat, about skidding off the road, about the snowplow driver who picked me up and dropped me off at the New Plat Motel, where it cost $27 for a room and $8 for a breaded veal cutlet dinner that tasted like turkey.

"The cat's taken a turn for the better, then?"

"Sure, sure," I said. "But I had to leave him in my car. The guy running the plow was allergic."

"I see," Jorg said. The Navy drained from his voice. "I hope he didn't freeze."

"Freeze? I never thought of that. Wouldn't his fur protect him? Isn't that why they have fur?"

In a panic, I called all the wreckers in town. Everyone in New Plat was in a ditch. I paced the floor. I took a long hot shower, and stood for an hour under the heat lamp. I paid $5.50 for an unsavory breakfast, keeping strict accounts to bill Priscilla properly.

The tow truck picked me up at noon. We drove out to my car. The car had attracted a small crowd of people from nearby houses. A state trooper was busy trying to jimmy the door. Some dog pissed on my tires.

"Don't open that door!" I yelled.

The dog bristled, started barking.

TRAGIC NEWS. STOP. ISAAC SCARED/FROZEN TO DEATH. STOP. HEARTFELT CONDOLENCES. STOP. ASHES ON WAY.

"I'm answering a complaint," said the trooper.

"Cruelty to animals," yelled a bystander.

"He's one of those scientists from the college," said another.

"Performs live experiments, I'll betcha."

"Isaac?" I cupped my hands on both sides of my head so I could see inside the car. I was relieved to hear him yowl. "Listen, folks, I'm an English teacher not a scientist. That cat was dying, and if it hadn't been for Dr. Flexnor. . ."

The magic name. They passed it around as if it were a holy relic.

"Flexnor's the best there is."

"A saint if there every was one."

"He's the kindest man."

"But expensive," I said. "Cost me 280 smackers to fix this cat."

Cold silence. The wind licked snow off my car and hurled it back into the ditch.

"He's not mine," I said.

That didn't help. The crowd dispersed. The wrecker hauled my car out of the ditch. The driver unfastened his hooks and cables. The dog barked nonstop. Isaac growled. The trooper sauntered over. "You didn't really pay that much for that cat, did you?"

The tow truck driver presented his bill.

"Fifty bucks?" I shouted. "What is this, the Big City?"

As I drove home to Winfield in a world gone white, the heater revived the assorted ingredients in my car. Like medieval devices of torture, the odors forced their way into the bones of my skull. I opened the side vent. Isaac was immediately on my lap, then he was trying to push his head, encased in the cone, out the window. I grabbed his tail. He hooked his front claws on the side view mirror and pushed off with his hind feet. I swerved to the edge of the road, veered into oncoming traffic. Drivers honked, waved fists, then smiled when they saw the cat. I pulled over and yanked him in. I rolled up the window, burying myself alive in the stench.

After a hot soapy shower, I called the student job service. I'm sure I didn't win any fans among the student body and I know a nasty account of the incident sits somewhere in my dossier, but the car had to be cleaned and I had no intention of doing the work myself, or paying for it. Later, I added up the bills (car cleaning, vet, motel, dinner, breakfast, telephone, towing, mileage), made copies, and mailed a set to England.

Priscilla called several days later. "How's Isaac?"

"He's OK."

"That doesn't sound awfully promising," she said.

So much depends on an aptly chosen phrase. But at that point I was pissed. Isaac's hit rate in the kitty pan hovered around 45 percent. The house reeked.

"Richard," she said, "you can be honest with me. How is he, really?"

"He's been a great deal of trouble," I said.

"Is he very demanding? Perhaps, if I came home, I could help out."

I nearly swallowed the receiver. She would disrupt her sabbatical, disrupt me, and spend a $1,000 just to fly home? I told her to save her money, Isaac was fine. His appetite had improved, he was getting used to his collar, I didn't mind the extra trouble. Honest.

"You're sure, Richard?"

"Priscilla, would I lie?"

The truth was I didn't want Priscilla underfoot, and I didn't want her to see the steps I had taken to combat winter's newest onslaught. I had covered the windows with plastic and covered the plastic with blankets. I had covered the doors of the rooms I wasn't using with blankets. I had closed off Isaac's room because the rug was beginning to stink. I had replaced all the bulbs in the house with 25-watters; I had lowered the temperature in the hot-water heater, and had turned the thermostat down to 50.

"Why don't you buy a few more kitty pans and set them in strategic locations. I'll reimburse all your expenses."

"Have you received the bills I sent you?"

"The check's in the mail," she said.

I bought two extra pans. Isaac continued to piss wherever the notion took him. When he wasn't furiously moving kitty litter from the pan to the floor and emptying his bladder, he sat on the radiator outside his room. Confident that nothing could be wrong with him now, I spent most of my waking time in my office—making headway, at last, on my chapter, rubbing elbows with my colleagues.

"Euthanasia is clearly the most humane course," said Flexnor, prodding, poking, jabbing his fingers and instruments into Isaac's unresponsive body.

"Quit joking. What's wrong with him now?"

Flexnor yanked out the thermometer. "Cats sometimes give up the will to live."

"It was that goddamned operation, wasn't it!"

St. Francis of New Plat shook his head emphatically.

What the hell was I going to do now? It was too late to tell Priscilla her cat was croaking (not after I had told her he was mending), and it was too late to announce the sudden demise of the English Department's mascot. The Department would confuse poor animal husbandry with my ability to teach Freshman Comp.

"What should I do?"

"You can put him away now, or you can wait three days, come back, and put him away then."

"I'm going to sue you," I said.

"I understand your bereavement," he said.

Back from New Plat, I wasn't in the house 20 seconds before the phone rang.

"Richard...?"

"Gail? I can't hear you. Speak up."

"Can you hear me now?"

"A little better. What did you say?"

"My plane arrives in Minneapolis on December 7th, 10:30 a.m."

"That's the day after tomorrow. Ten days early. Great."

"I'll take a cab to Winfield."

"No problem. I'll pick you up."

"Don't you have classes?"

"Screw classes, I'll be there. Can you stay through January?"

"Is Isaac that sick?"

"Gail?"

"Priscilla Crett, Richard."

I begged her not to come, told her Isaac wasn't that bad, that Gail would be visiting... She wouldn't listen. She'd take a room in the motel, if necessary. She felt obligated to help out because she had abandoned him.

I called Flexnor. Isaac was in heaven.

I immediately drove to Minneapolis, took a room at the Aqua City Motel, hauled out the Yellow Pages, and began calling every pet shop in town. I had to provide a replacement for Isaac and pray that Priscilla, full of love and anxiety, wouldn't notice the difference. But no one in the Twin Cities was selling full-grown Persians. Kittens were going for about $75 a paw. When I ran out of pet shops, I ran through the newspapers. Ten calls later, I had two leads: a four-month-old male and a half-breed female. The former was a big kitten, the latter was half blue, half white. I begged the owner of the half-breed for information about full-grown blue Persians. I offered her money. She said she had a pregnant female.

"Rent her to me for five days," I said, the moment I arrived at her home. "I'll pay $50 a day—$250 total."

She looked at me sideways.

"My girlfriend, actually my fiancée, is coming to town, and I want to make sure she's not allergic to Persians. I'm planning to buy her one for Christmas. You see, my old Persian just. . .just passed away. . ."

She patted me on the arm. I wrote out a check for $250, showed her my driver's license, and wrote down my address and telephone number. She fetched the cat. "Her name is Portia," she said, "Please be good to her." Portia was a dead ringer for Isaac.

Back at school, Jorg was glad to hear that Priscilla would be in town. But he cast a cold eye on my missing class to pick her up.

"What's wrong with Isaac?" Ms. Thayer asked when I ran into her on my way to my car and the airport.

"Nothing at all. Isaac's just fine."

"Then why's Priscilla coming home?"

"Cat lovers," I sighed.

"Cheer up, Rich. I got my Fulbright."

"Am I your replacement?"

"Aren't you going to congratulate me first?"

"I'm sorry. I'm really out of it these days."

"They're discussing it now."

"My being out of it?"

"No, my replacement. Quit worrying—you're a shoo-in."

As I waited for Priscilla's delayed flight to arrive, I couldn't quit worrying. How long would I stay a shoo-in if Priscilla or the English Department found out about Isaac? The thought of it turned my stomach an unpleasant color.

"Are you all right?" Priscilla asked.

"Cat care," I whispered. "It hasn't been easy. But he's mending. I'm afraid my school work has suffered, not inordinately, but. . ."

"That's our fault, entirely. I'll explain everything to Jorg, Rich. Rest assured."

But I couldn't rest assured, even when she remembered the check she owed me. She apologized for forgetting to put it in the mail, but promised to settle our account as soon as we arrived home.

"And the house," I said. "It's a mess."

45

She waved a hand in a "rest assured" manner.

"And Isaac. He's not as spry as he used to be. His nipples seem to protrude a bit and he's fat. Flexnor says it's a reaction to the antibiotics. You won't recognize him."

"I understand," Priscilla said. She ran into the house, cooing his name. When Isaac did not appear, she pushed aside the plastic covering his door and walked into his room. She stepped on and shattered a frozen mouse. She walked into Bart's study, then into her own. She ignored the glistening hoarfrost that coated their books. She smiled gallantly, said she understood when I told her it was easier for one person to live in two rooms. "We have to preserve our fossil fuels," I said. And I assured her that when Gail arrived, we'd open things up.

Priscilla flipped on the lights; the low-watt bulbs illuminated the dirt and grime. She walked into the kitchen, her shoes went thwick, thwick, thwick on the gummy floor. From the dish-choked sink she pulled out a saucer. She curled her nose over the sour milk, and slammed the refrigerator door to keep the mold from crawling out. She called, "Kitty, kitty, kitty," in a shrill falsetto.

The phone rang. Hoping it was Jorg with job news, I grabbed the receiver. "Hi, it's me. Guess what? I got all of January off."

"Sweetie!" Priscilla sang, reaching down to scoop up her beloved, who crawled out from under the sofa.

"What's that?" Gail asked.

"Darling treasure!" Priscilla crooned, dancing Isaac across the room.

"What's going on, Richard? Another class at home?"

"No, no, that's Priscilla, Priscilla Crett, the woman who owns this house."

"She's in England, Richard."

"I know, I know. But she flew back to nurse her cat."

"My pet, my precious," Priscilla cooed, kissing loud.

"Sure thing, Richard." Gail slammed the phone dead.

When Priscilla's noisy joy subsided, I picked up the phone to call Gail back. Ms. Thayer was on the line. She told me that Jorg would call at any moment, that the Administration rarely turned down his requests. She then spoke to Priscilla who offered abundant sabbatical, travel, and cat news. I twiddled my thumbs and whistled unpleasantly. I called Gail. She didn't answer. "You're ruining my love life," I told Priscilla.

"Don't worry, I'll explain the situation to her. She'll understand."

I hoped Priscilla was right.

Jensen the medievalist called to say hello, how's England?

Bart from London was next on the line, asking after Isaac's health. "Fat and lazy," she told him. "Rich has done an excellent job."

I could have purred with contentment.

Priscilla apologized when the phone rang for the fourth time. She handed the cat to me.

"Happy to see Mommy?" I said.

"Hello?" Priscilla said. "What? The cat's fine, thank you. No, I'm not allergic. Of course not. Portia? Who is this?"

I should have jumped up. I should have grabbed the receiver out of her hand, but I was across the room, savoring my victory.

DEAR ABBY

My name is Palmer. I live in Goshen, under a red tile roof in my father's stucco house, enclosed by English poplars, groomed hedges, and a brick wall ten feet high. My father is rich and irrational. In the 50s, he changed our name from Palmetto to Palmer. Later, he cemented shards of glass into the top of the wall. Over the years, the wall has protected my father from his illusory demons— thieves, murderers, escaped criminals, and madmen—but the wall has not protected the women in my family from the real demon—my father. Twenty years ago, my mother escaped him by driving off a bridge. Two weeks ago, my sister Florence took a long drive in the garage. Now my niece has been allowed to spend the winter with us. Nancy is fourteen and lovely, with dark brown eyes and long wavy hair.

Nancy and Don Lee, her father, brought Florence's body home to Goshen just before Christmas. Although the ground in the cemetery was harder than cement, my father insisted on a proper interment. Florence, he said, will not molder in cold storage until spring. For days the backhoe groaned and whined and scraped at the earth in the family plot in our backyard. On the day after Christmas, in the stabbing cold, we laid Florence to rest. The minister's teeth chattered as he galloped through the service. He grabbed at a chunk of frozen dirt, wrestled with it, broke it free, and tossed it at the coffin. The clod exploded into a thousand pieces.

After the service, we returned to the house where our Christmas tree blinked remorselessly. Every time the front door opened, the antique ornaments danced like bubbles in a bottle of champagne. Geoff, my attendant, parked me next to the tree, then walked back to the den to watch the Saturday afternoon fight. Everyone was crying but us. We were cried out. I smiled at the mourners as best I could, trying to nod when they touched my arm and whispered their condolences. The minister knelt beside me, rubbing his blue hands, asking me questions I couldn't answer without my alphabet board.

I watched my father preen in front of Nancy. She was telling him how empty the house had been without Florence. My father coaxed her to sit beside him on the couch where he hugged her like a loving grandfather. A moment later, he slid his pale hand across her leg, as if he were warming it up. When she giggled, he cooed softly like a pigeon. Like a pigeon, my father is short, dapper, and relentless. He is a fastidious little man, thin and delicate, who charms everyone he meets.

"Nancy," my father whispered, "have you ever been on a sleigh ride?" She shook her head. "Have you ever been on a toboggan or ridden a sled?"

I strained to hear what they were saying.

Nancy's eyes grew wide daydreaming of a white wonderland. A pair of gelded Morgans with golden manes pulled a baroque sleigh, a hundred bells jingled, and a million snowflakes the size of doilies drifted down through the still air. "I've never done any of those things, grandfather. It doesn't snow in Santa Cruz."

"You'd enjoy the winters we have here, Nancy. Your mother thrived on them." His hand strayed innocently to her inner thigh. "Would you like to stay?" he asked.

When Nancy nodded yes, I began rocking my head forward and back. My mouth opened, saliva began to drip on my sweater. The minister paused at the front door but thought better of wishing us a Merry Christmas. Behind him the sun glowed dully, a frozen egg yolk in a sky filled with white hills and windblown snow.

"Don Lee," said my father, cheery as a hawk about to be fed, "would you allow Nancy to stay with us until the summer?" My father casually removed lint from his black trousers.

50

Instead of saying, "You must be mad. Absolutely not. I wouldn't leave a cat in your care," Don Lee pushed the palms of his hands together and stared at his thumbs. Then he said, "Give me a moment to collect my thoughts, Edward."

I lost control. I jerked at my bell with my index finger, I smacked my lips. My head bounced around as if I were riding a runaway horse. My wheelchair creaked slowly forward across the marble floor.

"Are you OK, Palmer?" Nancy walked over and steadied my chair.

I stared at Don Lee, my head shaking and bouncing. Wasn't it obvious to him why my mother and sister had committed suicide?

Don Lee paced the floor, a hand at his cheek, his other hand holding his elbow.

My father stared at me. He knew what I knew. The little muff of hair that Edward Palmer called a mustache curled sourly. Clapping his hands, he called, "Geoff? Geoff, come take Palmer away."

Geoff ran into the room, spun me around, and wheeled me away. "This is some incredible fight," he said. He pushed me in front of the TV where two boxers were hammering at each other's heads. I continued to ring my bell. Geoff yelled, "Hey!" and when I didn't stop, he got up and ripped the bell out of my hand.

"Geoff, give him back his bell," Nancy demanded, her hands on her pubescent hips.

Geoff gave a quick look to make sure no adults were present, then he turned his back on her. She called his name repeatedly until he faced her again. His thick lips broke into a stupid smile; he stretched his arm out toward her, the bell dangling between his fingers. She grabbed the bell and hooked it into place under my left index finger. I rang six times.

"Geoff, what does six mean?"

Geoff watched the fight.

I rang six times.

"What does six rings mean, Geoff?"

Geoff waited until the round ended, then he said, "It means he's hungry. He's always filling his face. You know that."

I rang once, shook my head.

"Come on, Geoff, what does it really mean?"

"It means he wants his pointer and alphabet board." A cruel smile appeared on Geoff's face.

"Would you get them for me?"

"Sure thing, little lady."

Nancy confidently snapped the alphabet board into place across the arms of my wheelchair. She hesitated as she picked up the pointer. She studied the headband. I held my head rigid, but my mouth fell open as if I were yawning. She pushed the band down over my head; it ripped off hairs like a dull razor. I tried not to grimace. When she saw the pointer was aimed in the wrong direction, she twisted it around, nearly broke my neck. Geoff could barely contain his mirth; bubbles of nasty laughter broke out between his teeth.

"What's bothering you, Palmer?" Nancy asked.

I couldn't tell her my father had seduced her mother and would seduce her if she stayed here. I pecked at the alphabet board with my pointer, spelling out, "T-h-a-n-k-s, N-a-n-c-y."

"That's the big message?" she asked, squatting down in front of me. "Thanks for what?"

I spelled out, "Being friendly."

"I'm always friendly to you, Palmer. Besides, I can't cry anymore. I just can't, and I don't know a soul here except you and your father." She put her hands on my knees and looked up into my eyes. "Don't you want me to stay here with you?"

I spelled out, "Yes. Call Don L."

Pouting, Nancy pushed herself away. She reached into her dress pocket and pulled out a stick of gum. She tossed the wrapper at Geoff. Her soft lips sucked the gum in and her pink tongue rolled it up.

I rang my bell and spelled, "Please?"

She sat down next to Geoff to watch the fight. Geoff cheered noisily whenever one of the fighters landed a good combination. Nancy cracked her fat wad of gum, chewing like an imbecile. Then she walked back into the living room to talk to her father.

When Don Lee finally came in, I spelled out, "Don't let Nancy stay here with my father."

"Why not?" He moved in close, leaning over my chair.

I didn't know what to say. How could I tell him about his wife and his father-in-law? How my father had possessed her until she was married. How he had possessed her last summer for the first time in fourteen years. I couldn't tell him. I rocked in my chair. I strained against the belt that kept me from falling on the floor. I spelled out, "Because," then tapped my pointer on the board, while I thought of the right thing to say.

I could smell Don Lee's warm, milky breath as he hovered over me. "Take it easy, Palmer, and just spell it out."

"Say, could you go into Palmer's room," Geoff said. "I'm watching the fight."

I tapped at my alphabet board like a chicken gobbling grain. Don Lee stared into my eyes as if he were looking for water at the bottom of a well. Then my father walked in and said, "Don Lee, let's finish our conversation."

"He seems upset and wants to talk about something," Don Lee said.

"Come on," Geoff said. "I'm trying to watch the fight."

"He can use his word processor if he wants to talk." My father unfastened the alphabet board, then rolled my chair to my room; he pushed me in front of the word processor and switched it on.

I immediately pecked out, "Don't go away!"

"Don Lee's flight doesn't leave until tomorrow," my father said, throwing his arm around Don Lee's shoulder and guiding him deftly out the door.

How could I stop my father? Don Lee was a toady, the kind of man who always wears white cotton jumpsuits because ordinary clothes restrict and distract him. That's what he says. He says he once weighed three hundred pounds. Now he's slim and athletic looking. His straight black hair falls boyishly across his almond-shaped eyes. During his training as a psychologist, when he was still fat, Don Lee discovered that buried jealousy causes people to overeat. He wrote his dissertation on the subject. Today his fatuous treatment includes hypnosis, which helps his clients lose weight, and analysis, which uncovers the hidden jealousies that create the problem. His fast-food therapy has made him successful and wealthy. Fat people visit his clinic in Santa Cruz from all over the world—from Maine to Moscow.

I never criticized Don Lee's work in front of Florence. Don Lee had taken Florence away, away from Goshen and Edward. I was thankful for that. I just wished he were more engaging. He seems slow-paced, slow-witted, a touchy-feely type, who speaks slowly while he rubs and kneads you with his hands. If you ask him for an opinion—"What do you think of the President's foreign policy, the latest Novak novel or Sussman movie?"—he stares at you with those hypnotic, cow-like eyes of his.

"His mind works on a higher plane," Florence said, "beyond questions and answers and opinions. Just because he's not belligerent or argumentative like the Palmers, doesn't mean he's not smart. He's too smart to get into one of your power games, Palmer."

Too smart, I suppose, to notice his wife's and father-in-law's tryst. But last summer in Santa Cruz even Geoff noticed them, though he spent sixteen hours a day in front of the television. "It's the latest hookup. Fantastic programs!" he said. "I can't believe the things they get."

As far as I could see they got nothing but pornography. Geoff lapped it up, he glued himself to the tube like a leech on a cut. I could scarcely pry him away. When I did get his attention, he would moan, "When do I get a vacation?" Then he'd peel off my clothes, and change my diaper, and feed me, and wipe my face, all as fast as he could. Then he'd race back to the set.

When she wasn't in front of the television, devouring the garbage as if it were ambrosia, Nancy played electronic games in her bedroom, or lolled in the pool, swimming lazily and soaking up sun. The water on her skin highlighted the soft hollows and long muscles of her graceful legs, her firm high buttocks, her round breasts. Her nipples. No wonder Edward went mad for her after Florence died.

In Santa Cruz, he hovered over Florence, a harrier on the hunt, while Don Lee mesmerized eager clients in his clinic in town, and I stirred up the thick California fog. My finger locked on the control knob of my electric wheelchair (Edward hadn't disconnected it yet), I roamed from room to room, along the verandah, around the pool.

For days, awake or asleep, we lived in fog. The morning came slowly into focus, brightened for an hour or two, then slowly dissolved. Through the fog drifted Edward and Florence, arm in arm, hand in hand, like lovers who hadn't seen each other in fourteen years. Like young lovers, they didn't seem to care who saw them. I saw them everywhere: in the pool, by the hot tub, on the verandah. I saw them disappearing into the shafted light in the redwoods, where the cathedral silence was broken only by Florence's fecund laughter, echoing like bird song above the muffled rumble of the distant Pacific.

Geoff saw them. "Look at that, will you," Geoff said one day, coming up behind me on the verandah. A flight of pigeons sailed into a wild climb over the house and swept past Edward and Florence standing at the edge of Don Lee's estate. A red tail hawk drifted across the tree tops. "What a difference, huh?"

Even soft-brained Geoff was noticing the change in Florence. She had begun to glow, had become luminous, a flame inside a tall candle. When she met us at the airport she was drab and dull, Don Lee's wife— the queen of housework, duster in one hand, can of furniture polish in the other. She could barely manage sentences of three words. She would say, "That's very nice," or would ask, "You think so?" One day I asked her if she had seen any good plays lately. She said, "Nancy was in a school production of *Most Happy Fella*...." But in Edward's presence she began to burn—the old Florence, vivacious, clever, and witty.

"Are you happy?" I spelled out one day beside the pool, while the water nymph Nancy dove and danced and splashed tub-warm water on us. Edward, an alligator in the Nile, floated on a pink water mattress and flirted with Nancy like one of her gangly, pimply boyfriends.

"Intensely," said Florence. "What more could I want?" Nancy was yelling, splashing, demanding attention in the fractured water that slopped, slopped so softly, into the filter traps.

"But living in Santa Cruz is not like living in Goshen," Florence said. "There's no such thing as four seasons. It's monotonous. The fog's a bother. And from our house, it's a trek getting to San Francisco, where the traffic is dreadful and the parking nonexistent. You don't know how lucky you are, Palmer, to live so close to Hanover, where almost everything comes to you."

I threw my head around, my mouth opened, a squeaky cry shot out of my throat. Florence knew that Geoff had settled into our house like a rotting disease. She knew I went nowhere nowadays, except to occasional boxing matches in Boston, or college hockey games, or horror movies. She knew that despite my electric wheelchair I couldn't open doors, couldn't get down the front steps, couldn't get into or drive the car. She knew that when Mrs. Benson cared for me, I was in heaven. She encouraged me, took me everywhere, talked about everything. We saw the finest plays, movies, and concerts. Mrs. Benson read to me constantly. Florence knew that the only thing Geoff reads is the "Dear Abby" column in the newspaper. "Listen to this," he says, and whether I want to hear it or not, he starts telling me about the lady who sent thank you cards to her in-laws, addressing them Ms instead of Miss or Mrs. Did she make a Ms-take? "The Texas Chain Saw Massacre" was the last movie Geoff saw; he forced me to see it with him. Florence knew that Geoff makes me watch the soap operas because he likes to talk about them afterward. If I refuse, he parks me in my room in front of my word processor. Sometimes he turns it on for me, sometimes he doesn't.

Florence knew all my anguish because I wrote and told her, yet she defended Edward: "I'm sure he wasn't paying attention to Geoff's intellectual capacities when he hired him, Palmer. Dad was desperate to get someone." Desperate, she meant, to carry on with her full time, as soon as he buried mother and forced Mrs. Benson to retire early.

"You must be getting out more, now that you're. . ." Florence smiled, "...electrified." She laughed. She threw her arms around me and hugged me until the tears filled her eyes and wetted my cheeks. How could I despise her? What Edward had done to her wasn't her fault.

Over Florence's shoulder I could see Edward watching Nancy dry herself, dab her ankles and knees with a white towel, push the soft cotton into the diamond-shaped hollow between her inner thighs. Edward lowered his sunglasses when he saw me watching.

"Palmer," Florence whispered, "when I think how you must suffer. . ."

I threw my head in huge awkward arcs, first up, then down. I tried to smile, tried not to cry, tried to close my mouth so I wouldn't look as if I were yawning. But my mouth fell open and saliva dripped down my chin onto my alphabet board. I spelled out, "How miss what haven't had?"

"I miss Hanover and Boston," she said wistfully.

A few days later she and Edward drove off to San Francisco for several days of theater and museums. While I pitied him, Don Lee patiently explained to me how the awful traffic and terrible parking required their spending two nights at the Ritz.

But instead of sating them, their fling inflamed them. They carried on publicly, unmindful of Don Lee or Nancy—who had just turned fourteen. I discovered them the night Geoff abandoned me in front of my word processor, in my shit- and piss-filled diapers. I went looking for him, wanting him to change me and put me to bed. I pushed my control knob and rolled into the living room. I heard voices, whispers, musical laughter. The television? I turned my head—such a delicate word for what I do—I jerked my head right, up, down, sideways, right. A shaft of fluorescent light and a quavering of soft moans sifted out from beneath the den door. In the morning, the den would smell of sweat and semen. I jerked my head left, up, down, sideways, left. There was my father and Florence, wrapped together, mewing softly. I saw my father's silver hair, his straight shoulders beneath his silk smoking jacket, the heels of his black shoes; he was kneeling in front of the peacock-upholstered sofa upon which Florence, as if she were the naked Maja, lay clad in a white gown, open at the neck. I couldn't see the rest of her torso because his body blocked the view. I could see her bare white knees and her toes, painted red.

I smacked my lips. I pushed the knob forward, aiming for Edward's back. The electric wheelchair whirred maniacally, chewing up the space between us. Florence screamed, Edward smashed head first into the backrest. My restraining belt broke, and I jerked forward, sprawling on top of them.

After that Florence dimmed like a candle under a glass jar. To cover a sudden sprouting of blemishes, she dabbed a pasty make-up on her face and rouged her cheeks heavily. The next morning at breakfast, she tapped the crown of her soft-boiled egg and said, "Palmer, that was a pretty cruel thing you did to father." She pried away the jagged cap; the thick yolk overflowed the shell.

"Cruel, dear?" Edward asked, sitting down at the table. He began slathering butter on a croissant.

"Palmer's smashing into you," Florence said.

"Despicable," said my father, eating croissant. I pushed my control knob repeatedly.

"That's right," said Edward, "I disconnected your chair. We can't have you acting out the imaginings of that teeming brain of yours, now can we?"

Nancy wandered in and stared at the three of us, who were suddenly silent as statues. She picked up a croissant, slid it flake by buttery flake into her mouth.

I rang my bell. Nancy eased the croissant out, looked at me.

I rang my bell six times.

"What's that mean?" Nancy asked.

"He's a bother, darling," said Edward. "Don't pay attention to him."

I rang six times, paused, then rang six times again. "It must mean something, grandpa."

My father reflected for a moment, then said, "It means he's hungry." He turned toward the den. "Geoff? Would you come feed Palmer?"

I rang my bell six times.

Nancy stuffed the croissant back into her mouth, chewed quickly, then sucked her fingers clean. "I'll feed you, Palmer. Would you like that?" She ran her moist finger down the side of my cheek.

I tried to control my head, tried not to look disgusting or vulgar. I rang my bell six times.

Geoff was rolling up his sleeve as he marched into the kitchen. "You know he's been a real pest, Mr. Palmer. I don't see why we took him along. He doesn't enjoy himself. He just moans and groans constantly—"

"That's enough, Geoff. Feed him. He's hungry."

I started to throw my head around, left, right, up, down, forward, back. I rang the bell six distinct times.

"Six doesn't mean he's hungry, Mr. Palmer."

"Just feed him, Geoff."

I rang six times.

"Do you want a croissant?" Nancy said.

Florence whispered, "Edward. . ." and put her hand on his arm. I rang my bell six times.

"Feed him, goddamn it!" said my father. "He's always hungry."

Munching another croissant, Nancy watched as Geoff finished rolling up his sleeves and got down to business. I tried to keep my head level, tried to keep from gagging, tried to chew properly like a human being. But what happens is I throw my head back, my mouth falls open, Geoff shovels in the food, my head snaps forward, food spews out, my mouth closes, I chew and chew. I swallow. Sounds explode volcanically from my larynx, milk dribbles out my nose, some food goes down. My head flies back, my mouth falls open. Eager to get back to whatever show he's watching, Geoff fills up the serving spoon and shovels it in. Soon I'm covered with food that sours slowly throughout the day.

Don Lee came in and drew their attention away from me. He kissed Florence on the neck and patted Nancy on the behind. Florence buttered her croissant with fixed intensity. Geoff wiped my face as hard as he could and scuttled back to catch his favorite game show.

Don Lee, Florence, and Edward talked about the fog, about our going home, about how wonderful our visit had been. "We must get together for Christmas," said my father, taking his daughter's hand. Bored, Nancy wandered off, trailing buttery crumbs behind her.

The moment Nancy left the room, Florence turned to Don Lee. "Must you pat her like that?"

"Like how?" Don Lee said.

Florence averted her eyes.

"My back's simply killing me," Edward said, rubbing the spot where my knees had rammed him.

"You don't have to do that," Florence whispered.

"What's gotten into you?" said Don Lee as the dark fog pressed against the windows.

Don Lee contemplated the Star of Bethlehem at the top of our Christmas tree. Edward strutted back and forth, his hands behind his back, fingers twitching nervously. The mourners had gone at last.

"You wouldn't believe this fight," said Geoff, running into my room. "The Hammer's killing the son of a bitch. Want to see?"

I shook my head. From my room, I watched Edward pursue his quarry, inflamed by Nancy's luminescent flesh. "I believe it would be beneficial for Nancy to stay with us. Not only for a new experience, Goshen in winter, but also for a host of others, both physical and emotional. What's your opinion, Don Lee?" He patted Nancy on the head like a grandfather. "Nancy needs a change of environment. School, it seems to me, is of secondary importance. What do they learn in school nowadays? Computers?"

Geoff ran back to his fight.

"The only stumbling block, really, is school," said Don Lee. "We'd have to make some provision."

Edward picked a thread off his cuff. "We'd hire a tutor, Don Lee, that goes without saying."

I kept hoping Don Lee would be smart enough to see through Edward's sham of grandfatherly love. Instead, after another moment's consideration, he said, "That sounds fine to me." He turned to Nancy. "Nancy, the final decision is yours."

I could tell my father hated leaving the decision to a child. He paced nervously.

"I'd like to try something different, father," said mature, little Nancy, who a moment before had been playing hopscotch on the marble squares.

Geoff raced back in. "The Tiger's out cold. They're working on him, but it's like trying to revive a punching bag."

"Good, she'll stay here!" Edward rubbed his hands together in preparation for the tender feast. "I'll have the cook prepare something special for dinner." Then, like an old world gentleman, Edward kissed Nancy's hand and slid his fingers around her waist. Pale ghosts, his manicured fingernails danced over her black dress.

"I hope he doesn't expect me to pick up after her," said Geoff, staring past me into the living room.

I rang my bell and spelled out a message.

"Mr. Palmer," Geoff yelled, "he wants to talk to Don Lee."

As Don Lee walked into my room, I immediately began tapping at the keyboard; neat and orderly, the letters lit up on the screen: "Don L. you've been deceived. Flo. and Edw. had affair for years. Hard, yes, but face it before letting Nan. stay here. Edw.'ll do to her what he did to Flo."

Don Lee read what I had typed and chewed it over. He didn't gag, didn't even swallow hard. It went down as easy as salmon mousse. I had feared he'd smash the keyboard over my head or strangle Edward on the spot. He turned his black eyes on me. "Palmer, why don't you tell me how you're feeling?"

I tapped out, "Afraid for Nan. Only 14. Edw. will debase her. Nan. end up like Flo."

"I see," said Don Lee. He mulled it over, slow and steady, staring at me with those soft, melancholy eyes. "What I hear, Palmer, is a lot of trapped and projected anxiety. Why don't you drop the morality issue for a moment and tell me how your gut feels."

I stared at my terminal where the cursor blinked on and off. Don Lee patted me on the arm as if it were an old dog. He wasn't surprised, shocked, or revolted, and he didn't seem particularly concerned for Nancy's safety. I didn't want to think what I was beginning to think. But then I remembered the scene at the breakfast table in Santa Cruz when Florence and Don Lee fought over the way he had patted Nancy. The pat looked innocent to me. But Florence recognized it for what it was. She couldn't face herself reflected in her daughter. So she killed herself. It finally made sense. A green chill, like cold fog, pressed down across the nape of my neck. I felt nauseous. I was going to be sick.

Don Lee peered at me as if he were driving through a blizzard. He rubbed my arm as if he were kneading dough. "Palmer, it's easier to talk about these things if you say how you feel. If you put it off on someone else, you'll never deal with your problem."

I typed out, "You're worse than father. Can't help himself, but you condone—" I shook my head back and forth; the pointer rattled the keys on the board.

"Palmer," he said. He took my face in his hands. "Palmer, why don't you stop projecting your jealousy and frustration? Why don't you admit you're in love?" His face filled with a meaningful empathy. "Admit you're in love, Palmer, while you have the chance."

Love? Was that what he called it? Whatever muscle control I had disappeared. My head flopped, my jaw fell open, my pointer hit the enter key and my words zipped out of sight. The cursor blinked in black space.

"Come on, Palmer, let's not be so dramatic. I've watched you. You can't take your eyes off Nancy. You're jealous of anyone who comes near her. You snort and sigh when her boyfriends come round. You're frustrated, so you've twisted your feelings in knots. I can guess what you imagine. I'll bet you feel sorry for yourself because you're handicapped. And you're up to here with self-pity and hate. Right? That's OK, Palmer. You can feel, you can touch, you can communicate. Palmer, you don't have to live without love. But first you have to drop the moral baggage and admit your feelings."

I typed, "I'll never admit to your notions of love."

"Palmer," he said, "I know it hurts. I can't imagine what you've suffered." His eyes filled with tears. He placed his hot hand on my arm while he thought it over. "I know. I'll tell Nancy. She'll be happy to know you care so strongly about her." He smiled and stroked my arm. "She's much more mature and experienced than you think, Palmer. She's not just a little girl, though sometimes she acts it. And I know she's fond of you. She told me just the other day." Again he smiled. "Get to know her, Palmer. Let go of your anger and jealousy."

I shook my head, no, no, no, no. My pointer flew in a hundred directions at once. I wanted him to shut up. I wanted no part of his jealousy theories or his immorality. I wanted no part of Nancy. I worked the pointer off my head. It bounced across my legs and clattered on the floor. Don Lee smiled and folded his arms. He shook his head back and forth, his face full of sympathy. I knew exactly what he was thinking: How could I stop Nancy if she stole into my room one evening, and then, bending gently over me, pressed her phosphorescent skin against my wet, trembling lips?

OBIT

The cold rain glistened on the dark streets. Springtime in Goshen. Dawn was still a mountain range or two away. From my house on Pleasant I walked down to the hotel on Main. My boss had just called me up. "Frenchie's in trouble," she said. "You'd better get on it, Charlie." Frenchie lived at the hotel, one of the town's historic monuments.

In front of the hotel, the boys from the Fast Squad rushed a bagged corpse on a stretcher toward the ambulance. I saw that Ephraim and Sinclair were crying, and I knew Frenchie's troubles were over.

"When did he go?" I asked.

Ephraim's Adam's apple bobbed up and down like a frog in a jar.

Sinclair, his face wet from tears and drizzle, whispered, "Hour ago, maybe two."

"Too bad," I said. Cold water dribbled down my neck between my back and my shirt, raised gooseflesh on my shoulders. I asked if I could take a look, then unzipped the bag. Frenchie didn't look like a million bucks. His eyes were closed, the lids gray and wrinkled; his mouth was sunk in, his teeth were missing; his nose, full of long gray hairs, stuck out like the beak on some exotic bird. "Too bad," I said, zipping the bag closed. The zipper caught on Frenchie's diamond tie pin, a big stone, probably worth a year's salary. It seemed a shame.

The minute I cleared out of the way, Ephraim and Sinclair went back into overdrive, as if the Fast Squad had to live up to its name, no matter the patient's condition. They rolled the stretcher into the rear of the white ambulance. They slammed the back doors, climbed into the cab, slammed the side doors, gunned the engine, made the siren wail. They drove off into the night, the beacon whipping its red beam across the darkened store fronts.

I walked up the hotel steps. Ten people were pasted like leaves against the big wet windows. In the lobby, another twenty people milled around, looking wooden, dazed and sad. Frenchie's funeral had already begun. I had three days to write the obit. All I needed was the time of death and the date and time of the service. I had enough material on Frenchie Curts to fill the paper three times over. As I worked my way toward the elevator, the night clerk intercepted me. "Can I talk to you, Mr. Marlow?"

"Later, Daryl."

What I didn't need now was more human interest—how Frenchie sent me to college or turned my life around. "Who's in his room—Doc Murdock?"

"Sheriff Boggs," said Daryl. He was muscular and curly-haired. During the ski season, the girls sneaked behind the front desk to his shabby room and sway-backed bed.

"Thanks. I'll be back." I could see Daryl's plans for the night had been wrecked. He had probably been right in the middle of some honey when the ambulance arrived, the beacon whirling, the siren wailing as if the end of the world had come.

I climbed the stairs to Frenchie's room. Orville Boggs was kneeling on the floor, one hand stretched in front of him, a finger tracing the bloodstain on the rug.

"Sheriff," I said.

Boggs slowly pulled himself to his feet and tugged his cap low so I wouldn't see his red eyes. "Murdock was just here, Charlie. Said Frenchie had a hemorrhage. Wasn't anything anybody could have done. Guy across the hall heard him hit the floor." Boggs cleared his throat and wiped his mouth, then stumbled toward the door like a seasick sailor going for the rail.

I lit a cigarette. Frenchie had lived in the hotel since 1946. By 1952, he could have lived in a palace, several palaces—one here in Goshen to keep an eye on his casket company, one in Switzerland to keep an eye on his money, one in the South Seas to keep an eye on his tan. Instead, he rented two big rooms and filled the rooms with good furniture. He could have retired young. Instead, he worked a sixteen hour day. He chaired the board of his company, Goshen Casket, and served on a dozen others. The whole time, he gave his money away to worthwhile organizations and individuals. He could have surrounded himself with doctors, nurses, cooks, and valets (though half the people in Goshen would have looked after him for nothing). Instead, he died alone in his room, hitting the floor so hard he woke Ralph Hargroves, the town drunk.

I poked around, looking for his teeth. They weren't beside his bed or under it. On his bureau sat two diamond cuff links and a gold ring that I pocketed for safekeeping. I figured Frenchie died undressing, getting ready for bed. In the opened drawer of the bureau, I found socks and underwear, his wallet, a pack of condoms (Was he still going strong at seventy-seven?), and two stamped envelopes. One was addressed to Madeleine Andrews in Los Angeles, the other to Nadine Rabin in New York (old lovers?). I assumed he wanted the letters mailed, so I put them in my pocket and went on searching. I didn't come up with anything until I opened the medicine chest in the bathroom. Frenchie's teeth grinned from inside a glass of water. A tiny air bubble rose slowly to the surface.

"He's going to need these," I told Daryl when I went back downstairs. "Half the state's coming to his funeral. Frenchie touched a lot of people's lives."

Daryl eyed the dentures, then began chewing a cuticle off his pinkie. "Have you got a minute now, Mr. Marlow?"

"Sure, what is it?"

Daryl looked at the lobby filling up with mourners. News of Frenchie's death was spreading through town like a bad case of flu. Daryl gave me a look as if he were a rabbit that had run into a fox. "Mr. Marlow, have you ever heard anything bad about Frenchie?"

"Bad, Daryl?" Calm and easy, I lit another cigarette. "Sure," I said. "Everybody's got a skeleton or two in his closet. I've heard some things about Frenchie. What have you heard?"

Daryl glanced at the silent crowd, then motioned me to follow him behind his desk to his back room. The room smelled of talcum powder and latex. It was lit by a small black and white TV, chattering to itself in the corner. "This is off the record, OK?" he asked. I assured him it was. "Last night, at about eleven o'clock, I was trying to talk this girl out of leaving town on the bus. We were back here when Frenchie comes to the door, yelling like a drunk, saying he has to talk to me. When I get everything squared away, I let him in. Mr. Marlow, he's an awful mess. His hair's wild, his eyes are bugging out of his head, he's coughing like a three-piece band. He's saying he has to tell somebody the truth before it's too late. Then he tells me that he's not the great guy everybody thinks he is. 'No sir,' he says. 'Do you know what I did? I abandoned my wife in Paris, the Nazis took her away, and then she died.'"

I blew smoke at the TV. "That's what Frenchie Curts told you?"

"I swear, Mr. Marlow. I thought he was raving drunk. I told him to sleep it off, and I helped him back to his room."

"Wanted to get back to the girl, huh?"

"No, Mr. Marlow, honest. I thought it was alcohol. If I had known he was going to die, I would have called the hospital."

"Nobody's to blame for Frenchie's death."

Daryl suddenly didn't look like a rabbit anymore. "I suppose he was talking crazy because of the hemorrhage."

"Could be. You let me worry about that, OK?"

"That's fine with me," he said. "Just fine."

We walked back toward the lobby where the thickening crowd made the atmosphere pulpy. The rain had quit; fog pressed against the hotel's windows. The street lamps looked like haloed shrouds.

"How come you decided to tell me?" I asked.

"I figured you'd find out anyway. You always do."

I clapped him on the shoulder. "So, what happened to the girl?"

"What?"

"The girl in the back room?"

He laughed. "I'll have to take the Fifth on that one, Mr. Marlow."

After talking to Doc Murdock, I went home. Breakfast was waiting for me on the hot plate. By this time the sausage links had rigor mortis and the oatmeal had turned into marble. The hot cross buns had lost their religion. In the den, dressed and ready for work, Maggie was catching the last of the Morning Show. Kevin was home from school with an ugly case of ringworm. He wandered around, adrift, playing with his electronic toy. "Is Frenchie OK, Dad?"

66

"I'm afraid not," I said, sucking a piece of sausage from between my teeth.

Kevin's machine made an electronic splat; the bad guys pounced on the good guys, there was a song and dance, then more beeping.

"He's dead?" Maggie asked at the den door.

"Hemorrhage. He didn't know what hit him." I went over and put the kettle on the burner.

Maggie sniffed back the tears, came over, and leaned against me. "It's a shame," she said. "It's a damn shame."

"You writing the obit, Dad?"

I nodded to Kevin and gave Maggie a hug. I wrote practically everything for the paper except the sports, so the question wasn't who but what. Even that wasn't much of a question, unless Frenchie's last-minute confession turned out to be true. If it was true, Emily Thurston, owner/editor of *The Goshen Opinion*, and Gene Basswood, business manager, would react like Kevin's electronic toy—lots of splats, songs, and dances. Emily would demand notarized verification; Gene would walk back and forth, shaking his head, a worried expression on his face, his bald spot shining under the fluorescent lights. "It's going to be bad for business, Charlie. It's going to be bad." But if I had the facts, Emily and Gene would print whatever I had to say about Frenchie—good or bad. They let me do what I wanted, and they kept their hands off my copy. That was the least they could do considering my pay, my skimpy raises, my chances for promotion, or a piece of the business. No chance. *The Opinion* had been family-run for a hundred and fifty years. Emily was a spinster, Gene was her nephew. I was an outsider from Boston. If Maggie hadn't been born in Goshen, Emily probably wouldn't have hired me.

The kettle started to whistle.

"Make a cup for me," Maggie yelled from the den.

On the TV, the Morning Show hosts swapped the latest news about the guy who murdered the psychologist but was let off because the psychologist taped the murder session without asking permission.

Crime pays, I was thinking, while I held one of Frenchie's airmail letters above the kettle's steaming spout.

"What are you up to?" Maggie asked.

"Steaming open Frenchie's letters."

"Charlie, that's against the law."

"What the law doesn't know wont hurt it," I said.

She glanced at the envelope. "Who's Madeleine Andrews?"

The envelope's flap unglued itself and rolled into a neat curl. "That's what I wanted to know," I said, pulling out the letter. While I read the letter, Maggie waited, eager to become an accomplice. "Madeleine Andrews is Frenchie's daughter," I said. "She and sister Nadine are about to inherit six million bucks. Ten million goes into a trust for Goshen and three more go to Father Bradley at Sacred Heart Catholic Church."

"I didn't know he had daughters," Maggie said, stirring milk into her coffee.

"Seems like Frenchie has two daughters and maybe a few skeletons knocking around in his closet." I folded the letter and slipped it into the envelope. I wrote down Madeleine and Nadine's addresses, then put the envelope under a book.

Maggie was halfway back to the Morning Show when she yelled, "Charlie, are you planning to write an exposé on Frenchie Curts?"

"I'm not planning to do anything until I know what's going on."

She started walking back toward me, mulling it over. "You know, Charlie, it's one thing to write about the plight of farmers or abusive fanatical religious groups, but if you write an exposé on Frenchie . . . Christ, we'll be on everybody's shit list."

"Maggie, I don't plan to write an exposé. But I've got some curious rumors floating around that need verification. OK?"

"I know how you work," she said, waving a finger. "But don't forget, I've got to live here, too. So does your son."

"Maggie, come on . . ."

"Anyway, Emily and Gene won't print an exposé."

"First thing, it's not an exposé. It's an obit. Second, they'll print anything I can verify."

"And if they don't?"

"Cut it out, Maggie."

"All right. But when the crap starts boiling over, I don't want you threatening to leave town like you always do. We're not moving to Boston until Kevin's out of high school."

"OK, I won't threaten."

"Good, and I don't want to live in a town where everyone hates me. So, can you drop it, just this once, please?"

"How can I drop it? It's my job."

"Easy. You mail those letters, and you write up a heartfelt obituary telling everybody what they already know—Frenchie Curts was a great guy."

"Do you cut corners at the library?"

"Don't give me that baloney," she said. She grabbed her coffee and headed for the den. I can always tell when I win a fight because the loser always leaves the room.

I called Frenchie's daughter in California. A dark chocolate voice said, "Hello, this is Madeleine Andrews." I said hello. She said, "I'm sorry I can't come to the phone now. When you hear the tone, please leave your name and number and I'll get back to you as soon as I can. Thanks for calling." On the tape, seagulls bickered in the background, waves splashed and swished across a beach. I left my name and office number. Then I called information to get Nadine's number. When I called her, her answering service forwarded my call to her office. Nadine's voice was as hard as a bowling ball. When she heard who I was and where I was calling from, she said, "If it's about my father, I'm not interested."

I had prepared a polite speech full of euphemisms and apologies. Now I didn't know what to say.

"You still there?" she said.

"Your father died last night, Nadine. I'm sorry."

"Save your pity" she said.

I took a breath. "I'm writing the obituary for the town newspaper. I need some information. Could you tell me when your father was born and where he grew up?"

A tire rolling over fresh-laid gravel, that was Nadine's laugh. "You want the real story or more bullshit?"

"The real story."

"OK, he was born in Paris in 1908, in the Marais. That's where all the Jews lived before the war. He took over his father's casket company in 1929, the year his father died. He worked hard to become successful. (That much I'll grant him.) The war was great for business, until the Germans began confiscating Jewish property and deporting Jews. My father was terrified he'd lose everything. My mother, her name was Inez, thought he was a coward. She was right. I was six at the time; my sister Madeleine was eight. One day my father sold the factory and abandoned us. Two days later the SS rounded up the Jews on our block. By the time Madeleine and I came home from school, most of the Jews in our building were out on the street. We could

69

hear mother screaming from upstairs: 'My kids. You can't take me without my kids.' We ran up, shouting, but a neighbor grabbed us and pulled us into her apartment. Then we heard them dragging mother, who was shrieking, downstairs. We heard a rifle butt hitting her head like a cement block hitting the floor. Then nothing. A week later my father's sister took us to her farm outside Paris. We were shipped to America where we grew up with an aunt and uncle. My mother survived the camps, but died of TB in a hospital in 1946, the same year my father bought out the Goshen Casket Company. In 1950, during the Korean War, he finessed the government contract that made him a millionaire. He was a good business man. Anything else?"

I was scribbling notes fast. "Did you ever see him again?"

"I didn't want to. Madeleine did. He'd send us checks. He sent Madeleine to the Actor's Studio."

"And you?"

"Yes, I went to Harvard Business School."

"You're saying your father was a coward who ran out on his family. But what was he afraid of?"

"I told you, he was afraid the Nazis would confiscate his factory."

"But why? He was a Catholic. Were the Nazis confiscating Catholic property?"

The receiver was full of long-distance cries and whispers. "He didn't tell you, did he?" She cackled. "That's just like the bastard."

I can see Father Bradley reading Frenchie's obit in *The Opinion* Thursday morning. When he finds out there's been another Jew in the church beside the one on the cross, his heart stops, he clutches his fists to his chest, then he goes down like a stack of black Bibles.

"It's all yours," Emily said as I come into the office. Emily, at the paste-up boards, was scraping old news items off the front page to make room for Frenchie's obit. She held a pencil crosswise in her mouth; her blond wig was off center. Waxed strips of news-print covered her black dress. Emily was tall and bony; things on or near her were always slightly askew. But she had done the unexpected—kept the paper going after her father died—and then the impossible—made the paper a success. The only thing she couldn't do was produce an heir. Today Emily looked overworked and frail; mascara streaks lined her eyes.

"Hope we have some decent pictures in the file," I said, and then, as if I were pitching a softball to Kevin, I asked, "What do you know about Frenchie's life, Emily?"

"Only that he moved here from France during the war."

"Did you know he had two daughters?"

Emily looked at me as if we had just met on a dark street in Roxbury. Her hand darted up like a flushed bird, covered her throat. "I knew he had relatives in California; he often flew out there. But I've never heard talk about daughters."

Gene walked in dressed in black. He tapped me on the shoulder with his index finger and said, "You should be in mourning like everybody else. Frenchie was a great man. He was the closest thing to a saint you'll ever see. I went to Dartmouth, thanks to him. Did you know that?"

"Yes, you've told me more than once, Gene."

"Gene," said Maggie, "did you know Frenchie had two daughters?"

Gene was straightening his tie, pulling it tight. "Oh, my God, has he been snooping around?"

"I'm a reporter, Gene. I don't make up news, I find it."

Gene sliced the air with his hand. "No way, Charlie!" He walked off toward his desk, his big shoulders slouched forward as if he had already put in a tough day's work. "We're not doing an exposé on Frenchie Curts." He nodded once as a kind of exclamation point, without the usual confirming glance at Emily. Then he began searching through the papers on his desk. "Where's the goddamn copy for the subscription drive?"

Emily came over and told me that anything I came up with would have to be verified, and I'd have to list my sources, and then we'd have to talk. I said sure thing, and dunked my head in the picture file, thinking maybe it'd be smarter to turn Frenchie's obit into a homey little photo essay, preferably without captions.

Around ten, Madeleine Andrews called and asked if I had talked to Nadine. When I said I had, she said, "I'll tell you the 'real story' if you pick me up at the Lebanon airport, 7:30, Wednesday morning."

I said sure thing, wondering if the real story would be better or worse than Nadine's?

Later, I went to the Goshen Cafe for coffee and doughnuts. The atmosphere at the restaurant was grim. Usually on a Monday morning you couldn't hear yourself talk. Now there was only an occasional sob and the clink of coffee cups and teaspoons. Mourners dressed in black filled every seat. Frost, the baker, was wearing a black apron over his white undershirt and white pants. He came over to the counter while his wife Joan worked the tables, making sure everyone's coffee was warm and no one lacked a doughnut or napkin. Frost laid his beer belly on the counter and leaned toward me. "Hell of a goddamn shame, isn't it?"

"You're not kidding," I said. I lay my hand on the counter and spread my fingers. "But you know, there's more to the guy than any of us suspected."

"Like what, Charlie?"

"You sure you want to hear?"

"Of course," he said, raising his voice. "Look, Frenchie was a great guy. Nothing he's done can change that. Whatever he did, he did for a good reason. I don't care what it was."

"Anything?"

"You're gonna tell me he gambled? Cheated on his wife? Charlie, nobody's perfect, right?"

"You've got a point, Bob," I said, and before he had a chance to ask me what Frenchie had done, I was out the door. I walked up one side of Main Street and down the other. I was beginning to feel about as comfortable as a snowman in August.

Tuesday I wrote up an obit that wouldn't ruffle a barb on a dove's feather. But it didn't feel right. I mentioned that "Frenchie Curts is survived by his daughters Nadine Rabin and Madeleine Andrews" so the town historian would have something to go on, if he or she noticed and wanted to follow the lead.

Wednesday A.M. I drove down to Lebanon to pick up Madeleine. She was tan, tall, and regal, the image of her father. Though she had flown the Red-Eye from Los Angeles, she looked fresh as this morning's jonquils. When we drove onto the Interstate, she lifted her sunglasses, opened her mink coat, and looked out across the Connecticut River Valley at the dark blue layers of hills. "He was a real Aries," she said, her voice rich as mocha. "But he was close enough to the cusp to make him interesting."

"Your father?"

She nodded. "Nadine told you he sold his factory and abandoned the family. Right? That's what she has to believe. Nadine was six, she didn't know what was going on. And Nadine's a real Capricorn. She sees everything in terms of buy and sell."

"And you?" I asked.

"A Libra."

"You're an actress."

"I act, but mostly I do voice-overs. You know what they are?"

"Sure," I said.

She looked off toward Mt. Moosilaukee's boulder-strewn summit. "Inez was a Taurus, a real bull. She was determined to maintain her rights as a free Frenchwoman despite the Nazis' threats to deport all the Jews in France. 'I am a citizen,' she used to shout. 'I have my rights. We can't let those barbarians bully us around.'

"'But we lost the war,' father would tell her.

"'We have a president. We have a constitution,' Inez would say. 'We are running this country, not the Germans.'

"I remember days and days of arguments, my father pleading with her. 'Inez, we'll just move the family to my sister's. The country will be good for the girls. I can run the factory from there.'

"'I am not moving in with your sister and her stinking husband. My girls are not growing up with cows and pigs. What kind of education would they get in that miserable one room school house?' My mother was a short powerful woman, with long black hair that she wore like a crown on the top of her head. She would tap on my father's chest with her index finger, underscoring her ideals, embodying them in physical action.

"'They'll deport us, don't you understand, Inez? They'll send us to Poland.' My father would shout, pull his hair, rush back and forth across the living room floor, an animal in a small cage. One time, I remember, he stopped pacing. He grabbed her hand, said, 'I'll prove it to you,' and dragged her into the Metro. They got off in the 17th Arrondissement, near the apartment of friends on the Avenue des Ternes. The avenue is lined with pruned trees that look like men marching, their arms raised in surrender. Their friends lived in a big building, its courtyard opened to the sky. My parents hadn't been there for months, but the moment they stepped inside they smelled beer and brats and sauerkraut—the stink of Germans. The crisscross clotheslines between the balconies were hung with brown shirts. The shirts looked like huge dark bats frozen in the air. The courtyard was strewn with litter, pieces of wood and cobble. In the old days it was spotless, swept every morning by the half-blind concierge who cared for the building as if he owned it. While my parents stood gaping, a guard walked up behind them. He was a big man, fat red cheeks, tiny nose, round double chins. The guard demanded identification. My father said he was looking for a business associate. He used a Christian sounding name. But the guard kept asking if he was a Jew. Inez stepped in and said, 'That's none of your business,' then she turned and walked away, tough as a snapping turtle. Outside, she told my father, 'Don't you see? They want to frighten us. They want us to scurry off like beetles so they can take over and turn everything into a pigsty.'

"Can you imagine? She would have stood up in front of the entire German Army and the SS and sung the Marseillaise."

"'Bambi Meets Godzilla,'" I said.

"Is that the one where the monster stomps the cute little fawn flat?"

I nodded.

"We would have all been Bambis if my father hadn't done something."

"I thought he abandoned you?"

She waved a hand in my face. "He did that only to scare my mother. As a last resort. To show her he meant business. He had tried everything else. He had his sister write letters to Inez, begging her to leave Paris. He fought Inez, pleaded, threatened, stood on his head. He even tried to kidnap us. But Nadine's whimpering gave us away. After that there was nothing left for him to do. He wanted to scare her. Twenty-four hours he was gone. The Gestapo arrived and dragged her and half the building off. Inez screamed about her rights as a free French citizen. She yelled about her rights until they knocked her unconscious. Her shoes squeaked down the steps as they dragged her away. From the window, we saw the front gate thrown wide open, the Gestapo's black car on the cobblestones, the heavily dressed men, women, and children marching off down the street toward the train station. An infant was bawling.

"When my father found out, he went crazy. He searched the train stations, he called friends in high places, the Jewish Council. They warned him to keep quiet. He sat for days like an animal with its leg caught in a trap. He sold the factory for practically nothing, took us to his sister's, then to America. I remember a night in a boat, cold and wet, bouncing on choppy waves, Nadine with a rag in her mouth; my father carried her like a sack of potatoes. We stayed with Aunt Ray and Uncle Harry in New York. She was fat and strict; he had huge round eye-glasses and looked like an owl. They were older parents, hard and distant. Father paid for our boarding schools, colleges, graduate schools, everything. He never stopped paying for leaving her."

Madeleine flipped her sunglasses down over her eyes, and leaned back. I thought maybe she was crying. The sky and the round green hills reflected on her lenses. After five or six miles, she said, "What are you going to do, Charlie?"

"I don't know. Nobody in town knows the truth. He left millions to the Catholic Church. Father Bradley will be surprised to find out he was a Jew."

"Surprised?"

"Yankee understatement. Everybody in town's going to shit."

"People don't have to know."

"But people ought to know."

"You receive the word direct from God?"

"It's a good story."

"But maybe it shouldn't be told, Charlie. Maybe it doesn't matter if people know the truth about my father. It won't change anything. He meant well, he made a mistake."

"So why'd you tell me the story?"

"I figured my father would be better off with my version of the truth than with Nadine's."

Which truth? Nadine's dark version? Madeleine's? Or Gene's? His version of the truth was rimmed with gilt, a twenty-piece brass band humped away at the Star Spangled Banner while he stood at attention, his hand over his heart.

We drove in silence, me wondering what in hell I was going to do, Madeleine probably wishing there was no such thing as the First Amendment.

When Goshen came into view up the Interstate, I pointed it out: the church spires, the white frame houses in tiers on the hillside, the dark brick building beside the falls.

"Pretty, pretty," she said. "When's your birthday, Charlie?"

"Can't you guess?"

"April 23," she said.

I nodded.

Madeleine started to laugh and couldn't stop.

"What's so funny?"

"Same day as Inez," she said.

I let her out in front of the funeral home. No one sitting vigil knew the tears on her cheeks were from laughter.

I drove straight to the office, walked into my cubicle, closed the door, and wrote a second obit, Madeleine's version, cutting and pasting the factual material I had already written and weaving it into the text. I figured it was my job as a reporter. I figured people expected me to be honest. If I didn't tell them the truth, they'd find out anyway; any of the newspapers in the area could write the story. I figured if that happened, I'd look pretty shoddy.

Maggie didn't see it that way. That evening, I ran the obit past her, but she stopped short at the first revelation: "Frenchie was a Jew?"

Kevin stood beside her, stuffing popcorn into his mouth, which was haloed with spaghetti sauce. "What's a Jew, Mom?"

Maggie told Kevin to go to bed. Kevin looked at me. I told him to please go to bed. The minute he hit the bedroom door, Maggie said, "Father Bradley will have a fucking coronary, Charlie."

"I don't think so."

Maggie glanced up at me. "You don't think so?"

"You haven't finished reading."

"I don't have to." She turned to me. "I know what you're up to."

I sipped Scotch. "I'm trying to report the news."

"Don't give me that freedom of the press shit. You've been milking that angle for years: 'Charlie Marlow, tough, incorruptible reporter for a small, local newspaper.' The truth is you do these exposés because they salve your conscience. You can say you're incorruptible and forget about your stagnant career. You've dead-ended yourself, Charlie."

"What you want is promotions and raises?"

"I want you to stop hurting people to make yourself feel better."

"The truth doesn't matter?"

"Sometimes it doesn't, Charlie. Drop it. Please?"

"And if I don't?"

"If you don't, maybe you shouldn't come home."

"Oh, Jesus Christ. You mean it?"

She didn't answer, but she didn't have to. Her face was shining with tears and she was standing her ground.

At five minutes to nine, Wednesday night, about three hours before we put the paper to bed, I handed copies of Frenchie's obit to Emily and Gene. I hadn't changed a word of it. I figured if you throw away your ideals, what's left? I told them I'd be at the Corner Bar, and I guessed Gene would roar in, his ears smoking, in about ten minutes, waving the obit as if it were a Molotov cocktail.

"Let's talk," he said, about thirty-five minutes later.

"Your place or mine?"

"You're a funny guy," he said.

Outside the sky had gone slate gray, the air smelled of manure, big fuzzy snowflakes whizzed down. Springtime in Goshen. I could tell something was up; Gene was too calm. I yakked about the weather, but Gene wasn't interested in making small talk. He had rolled his copy of the obit into a tube, and as we walked along he thumped it against his thigh.

At the office, Emily was sitting at her desk, surrounded by a sea of yellow copy. Nearby, a plastic fork skewered her half-eaten dinner. "I'm sorry, Charlie," she said.

"Don't be sorry," I said. "Paste it up."

"We can't."

"It's a great story, Emily. And I've got all the verification you could ever want. His daughter's right here in town."

"That's not the point."

"The point is," Gene said, "this is going to make enemies."

"You mean it'll ruin the subscription drive."

"I mean it's bad for business. Bad for you, bad for your family, bad for us, bad for Frenchie... You name it, Charlie, it's bad."

"Look, my job is to report the news fairly, objectively, impartially—regardless. That's what I've done. Now you hold up your end of the bargain and print it."

"Charlie..." Emily said.

"If you don't want to print it, I'm sure the papers in Lebanon and St. Johnsbury will oblige."

Gene raised his eyes toward the ceiling and exhaled slowly and noisily.

"Charlie," Emily said, "we understand your position. You're a reporter. You're a damn good reporter. We appreciate that. We appreciate the stance you've taken over the years. There were times we would have backed off, gone soft, but you kept us at it. Don't shake your head. It's true. You're one of the reasons we've become so successful." She paused. "Now hear me out, Charlie, I don't want you to misunderstand what I'm about to say."

"Please, don't bribe me, Emily."

"We want to make you an offer."

"Don't. . ." I said.

"We want to give you a twenty percent raise, enroll you in our profit-sharing program, and promote you to senior editor. I need help. We're swamped with work."

"That's very generous, Emily. I have to think it over."

Gene stared at me as if my ears had fallen off. "You're not bellowing," he said.

"Say you'll accept, Charlie." Emily said. "I'll edit Frenchie's obit."

I thought it over. I paced. I scratched my head. I made all the appropriate gestures. How could I turn down an offer like that? But then I began to feel queasy, shabby.

A big stupid grin, like a stepped on cow paddy, spread across Gene's face. He grabbed my hand and pumped it up and down, full of passionate intensity.

"I haven't said yes," I told him.

"But I think you will. I really think you will. Welcome aboard, Charlie."

"Congratulations, Charlie," Emily said, shaking my hand.

"Tell me," Gene said. "Did you engineer the whole thing so we'd have to make you an offer?"

"I'll talk to you in the morning," I said. "Good night."

I headed home. Then I stopped and started to walk back to the office. I stopped again. I stood there on the sidewalk for a long time. I'd tell them to go to hell in the morning. I watched the big beautiful flakes slap the wet sloppy street. All for nothing. It was springtime in Goshen. Nothing could stop that.

THE FALL

John's breath condenses into smoke. He pulls the blankets up to his chin. From the kitchen, Mary calls gently, like a swallow coaxing a fledgling out of the nest. John blows and scrapes a knothole in the elegant frost flowers blooming on the window next to his bed. He sees that one dark cloud covers the sky. Hoarfrost grins from the unraked leaves in the yard. In the garden, frozen pumpkins, like the heads of decapitated giants, lie scattered amidst the black-leafed vines. Mary calls, soft as distant birdsong: "John . . .? Please come down, make the fire." John yanks himself out of bed, jerks himself into his clothes, rushes downstairs.

Marcia sits on the playroom floor next to Russell, the dog, and a pile of naked dolls. The dolls stare like fish on ice, their body parts at odd angles. Marcia smiles. John pats her on the head, walks into the kitchen, pecks Mary on the cheek. He opens the plastic-covered screen door, walks through the woodshed into the lake of leaves in the yard. Tattered banners of fog rise from the Connecticut River Valley. The mountains of New Hampshire are capped with white enamel. John's breath billows thick as cigarette smoke. He wonders, What if someone saw me from the road, thought I was smoking, and reported me to the Elders? Would the Elders listen to the truth? John walks back into the woodshed and stares. Except for three logs, and two gnarled stumps shaped like gargoyles, some bark and twigs, the wood-shed is empty.

John stands in the kitchen clutching the wood. The cats twine in between his legs. Under the fluorescent light, John's face is pale, round and soft as fresh dough.

"We've run out of wood."

"Better call Mr. Farnum for some more."

"Didn't he just deliver a load?"

"In April. It's the end of October."

The oatmeal foams, bubbles, races upward, but Mary stirs it down with several gentle twists of her hand. She brushes the hair out of her eyes. Her face, wreathed by dark curls, glows.

In the living room, John shoves the kindling and the logs into the fire box. He lights the paper. As the kindling begins to crackle, John gazes at the exposed rafters. Dust-coated spider webs dance on the rising air.

In April, John tore down the old plaster walls and cheap paneled ceiling. Shimmering plaster dust filled the house for days. After a week's rest, John attacked the middle room, Marcia's playroom, pulling away the four layers of wallpaper and the horsehair plaster, exposing the rough-hewn lath, which immediately began to warp. (Now the laths stick out like the ribs of a martyred saint.) John planned to insulate, sheetrock, and wallpaper, but in May he discovered the Truth, and then Mr. Deuthson offered him a job at the Happy Hour Bar. From that moment on, his Bible studies and his job took up all his time.

Mary coughs and calls John's name. Black smoke curls along the ceiling into the kitchen. John closes the grate. He walks into the playroom, where Marcia is trying to push a doll's leg back into its socket. Shaggy and arthritic, Russell gnaws at a pock-marked doll as if it were a bone.

John goes to the phone and dials Farnum's number. He pushes the plungers, listens to the black receiver. "Something's wrong with the phone."

"I hope it's not disconnected," says Mary. "Did you pay the bill?"

"I'm sure I did."

Mary's bedroom slippers slap softly against her heels as she walks to the counter and begins looking through the bills in the drawer. Tails stiff, the cats rub and push against her ankles.

"I'll drive up to Farnum's," says John. "Tell him myself."

"Take the checkbook, John."

"He'll have to take an I.O.U., Mary. I don't get paid until next Friday." John throws on his coat and hurries out to the car.

"Lookin' for Lester?" asks Bessie Farnum. Shaped like a snowman, she fills the door. "Lester's yonder, tinkerin' with his Jeep." She lifts her thick arm to point across the yard.

John walks carefully over the rutted, frozen ground, passing Lester's RV, dump truck, dozer, tractor, skidder, and grader. He eyes the skeletons of eight abandoned Jeeps, models spanning thirty years, like a museum display showing the evolution of the horse.

"Damn this weather. It's the ups and downs lets the moisture in. Gas line's froze." Lester's shoulders are matted with frozen sand from lying under the engine. He chews a brown cigar butt. Lester reaches for the ignition switch; his beer-belly bumps on the steering wheel. He pumps the gas pedal; the engine chugs laboriously. Lester hauls himself off the seat, spits. "Goddamn goddamn!" He yanks the hood up and starts twirling wingnuts and removing blackened, gooey parts.

John sees smoke curling up around the engine, sees the fire of twigs Lester built under the oil pan to thaw the gas line.

"See your little rust-heap's still running," says Lester. "Didn't I tell you it was the best deal in town? Here, give me a hand." He grabs John's hand and pushes the meaty part over the mouth of the carburetor. Lester cranks the engine. The carburetor sucks and explodes but the Jeep doesn't start. "Goddamn cold!"

"Wouldn't it be nice," John says, "to live where it's always warm?"

Lester twists and rolls his dead cigar from the left to the right side of his mouth. He looks at the gray flannel sky. "I guess. But I can't afford to move." He rubs his gunky hands on his overalls. "Sides, everybody's moving South. Kind of a fad, ain't it?" He tries the engine again, it flops over slow like a dying fish. "Hell with it," he says, wiping his hands on a grease-stained rag. He tosses the rag to John who smears black gunk over his fingers. Lester points a finger at John, and a gap-toothed grin spreads across his face. "Say, you wasn't talking about moving South. You was preaching heaven—that's the only place it'd be warm all the time." Lester slams the Jeep door shut. "Came up here to save old Lester Farnum's soul, did you?"

Gooseflesh breaks out all over John's body as he realizes his faith is visible. Mindful of Scripture, however, John says, "I didn't come up here to save you, Lester. I came to ask you to deliver some wood."

"Could've phoned for that," says Lester, waving the oily rag at him. "Hell, I wouldn't mind considering the state of my soul, Mr. McAdam, but I know it's hopeless." Lester trudges off across the hummocky yard toward his house. "I was raised Baptist, you see, so I know how far I've strayed. Know what I figure? If the good Lord cared two hoots about this world, he'd have stopped things from getting as bad as they are."

John walks carefully, trying not to break his ankles on the frozen muck. "I don't know all the answers, Lester, and I'm not supposed to preach on my own. But I can tell you this: everything you see shaping up in the world was predicted centuries ago. We are in the midst of a terrible span in history, a period known in the Bible as the Great Tribulation. Do you know the Bible?"

"Oh, yes, sir. My Daddy whopped it into us," Lester lights a wooden match on his fly.

"Then you must be familiar with *Revelation.*"

"That was Daddy's favorite. Couldn't get enough of it."

"Then you know that Jehovah set forth step by step exactly how the world would end. The troubles in Europe and the Middle East, the wars all over the world—it's right there in *Revelation*, predicted thousands of years ago. And things are going to get a lot worse before they get better, especially for sinners. If I were you, Lester, I'd repent now, before it's too late."

"Repent..." says Lester. They reach the porch where Bessie has set out a row of grinning jack-o'-lanterns. Lester removes his cigar and taps it with his pinkie to see if it's lit. "Repent my sins..."

"Or live an eternity in hell," says John. "Repent and live forever in the Earthly Paradise, where it's always warm, where the sun always shines."

"I'd have to confess, wouldn't I?" Lester glances at the eviscerated pumpkins and stuffs his dead cigar into the eyehole of the one closest to the steps.

"You'd have to speak to Mr. Deuthson. He's a church Elder."

"No harm thinking about it, I guess."

John explains where to go and what to do, then reminds Lester that he needs the wood delivered today.

"Might just as well be prepared as not," Lester says.

Jehovah's radiance fills the gray sky. Dead leaves swirl down the dirt road behind John's car. Back at the house, John discovers the unpaid electric and telephone bills on the kitchen table.

"I must have forgotten to pay them, Mary."

"The electricity just went off."

"I'm sorry."

"We have to go, John. I can't be late for work again."

In the car on the way to town, Marcia marches her one-arm doll across the back of the driver's seat while John tells Mary what happened at Farnum's.

"We're not supposed to do Service calls, John. Not until we're baptized. That's what Mr. Deuthson told us. Even then, we're supposed to go with more experienced Witnesses. Never alone." Mary scrapes their frozen breaths off the windshield.

"I didn't preach, Mary. Lester almost came into the Truth himself."

Marcia winds her doll's arm around like the sweep hand of a stopwatch. Mary says she understands and scrapes. White shavings of frozen moisture drift through the car. Mary's eyes grow misty as John recounts the exhilarating moment they grasped Jehovah's plan and foresaw the glories of the Final Trump. At that splendid moment, Witnesses would gather together in perfect happiness to live on the Paradise Earth, where the lion and the lamb would lie down together, where peace would reign forever. One hundred and forty-four thousand of the Select would join Jehovah in heaven. With a pang John realizes that Mary will be asked to join that chosen group. John wonders if Jehovah will separate married couples. If married couples are separated, who would care for the children?

"John!"

John looks up, jerks the steering wheel. The car shoots back into the right lane.

"I think you should tell Mr. Deuthson what happened."

"It wasn't my fault, Mary."

"I know, John."

"I hardly said a word."

"Still, you'd better let Mr. Deuthson know."

The McAdams arrive in town. They pull up in front of the Goshen Day Care Center. A chain-link fence encircles the brick building and three dead elms, stripped of bark. At the front door stands Mary's boss, Mrs. Justin Dickey, who wears dark wool skirts and smells of crayons and cookies.

Marcia pushes her way out of the car, clatters up the porch, jumps into Mrs. Dickey's arms. "Here's my sweetheart," she croons, pulling the little girl into the folds of her skirt. To John she says, "Another nice day."

Mary kisses John good-bye, pats him on the arm.

John glances at the dark sky, full of hummocky clouds. He stares at Mrs. Dickey.

John drives south of town to the Happy Hour Bar on the Lower Plain. Mr. Deuthson is already at work, standing at the bar, polishing wine glasses with a white cloth. John ties on an apron and joins his boss beneath the rack, where the wine glasses hang down like transparent fruit. John tells Mr. Deuthson about Mrs. Dickey, "Does she mean 'Another nice day' like everyone else means it? Or am I hearing a hidden message?"

Deuthson holds a glass to the light. He is tall and thin and John must look up to see Deuthson's smile quivering at the corners of his mouth. "Already you perceive the community's hostility to our beliefs, despite their free-thinking philosophy, and their cherished Yankee independence. Your perception is correct, John. The Dickey woman is mocking your faith. Another nice day implies Doomsday has been forestalled. I am afraid, John, that as we near the Final Trump, we can only expect more mockery, ridicule, and persecution." Deuthson rubs his glass and sets it aside. He reaches up into the rack and pulls down a pendulous snifter, which he hands to John.

John rubs contemplatively. "Mary has to work for that woman."

"Mary is dutiful, she'll follow your example, John. All the Elders are proud of the progress you've made."

The men polish the wine glasses. Eventually, each glass squeaks with perfect cleanliness. Deuthson cleans seven snifters; John works diligently on three. "Something happened today. . ." John whispers, clears his throat, coughs.

Mr. Deuthson inclines his head in John's direction. To John it seems as if the liquor bottles and their reflections in the mirror have rotated their pour spouts to listen. John explains what happened at Farnum's while Deuthson eradicates smudges, fingerprints, the waxy blush of lipstick. When John finishes, Deuthson reflects quietly, his smile flickering at the corner of his mouth. He taps his glass; it rings a lovely, full note no human voice could match. "You see what a clever adversary Satan is?" He holds the glass to the light. "Satan can invest even sacred moments with his presence. Invisible yet omnipresent, like a filthy fingerprint on a seemingly clean glass. That's the Evil One, John." Deuthson twists the glass to reveal a half halo of red lipstick.

"But it seemed so natural, Mr. Deuthson."

"That's how the Devil works," says Deuthson, his eyes half-closed, nodding his head. "He leads you in, innocent, eager, fresh, without a care. Then he laughs because you think it seemed so natural. Yet there you stand in blasphemy." He pats John on the back. "Now you know why we insist newcomers wait a year before baptism and why we go out on Service in a group."

John stops wiping. "But why, Mr. Deuthson? If a lost soul needs saving before the light goes out...?"

Deuthson does not answer. He rubs his glass while the Happy Hour Bar fills, then overflows with John's reverberant question. Deuthson leans forward and taps the counter hard as if he were crushing ants. "Because it says so in Scripture." He smiles. "Your eagerness to spread the word led you from Scripture into the Wilderness. That's precisely where Satan wants you."

"Of course," John whispers, lowering his eyes, bowing his head. John could see the truth now. The truth had camouflaged itself like a bird's nest in a tree. Now that John could see it, he couldn't understand how he had missed it; nor could he not see it as he once had.

Deuthson's face glows like a pumpkin with a candle inside. He lists a dozen instructive passages from Scripture and advises John to study them carefully. "You needn't castigate yourself, John. With the excellent progress you've made, it won't be difficult to convince the Elders that only your eagerness led you astray."

"Elders?" John says, stuffing his dishcloth into the narrow throat of a chablis glass.

"The seven Elders meet on Monday evenings to discuss problems and guide the brethren."

John stares at his mud-caked shoes.

Deuthson claps John on the shoulder. "Be glad it's tonight. You won't have to wait all week for our decision."

"Will they," says John, "disenfranchise me, Mr. Deuthson?"

"No, no, John," says Deuthson, full of good humor. "Disenfranchisement is reserved for only the most serious lapses, for intractable cases. Your error is a tiny mote on an unblemished slate." Deuthson's face is now robed in a full smile, until he glances out the window and sees John's rusted car sitting beside the front door. "Run outside, John, and park in the back. I've said before, we don't want to attract the wrong clientele."

"I forgot." John rushes out in his shirt sleeves, despite the cold.

John tends bar through the Businessman's Lunch, cleans up, then drives home. In the east, the clouds have disappeared behind the purple mountains. In the west, the sky is filled with clouds shaped like huge balls of steel wool.

Lester's dump truck, loaded with wood, sits in front of John's house. John honks a Hosanna and parks beside his tumble-down barn. He finds Lester standing between the cab and box of the truck. Lester hammers at the dump lever with the back of his ax. Inside the house, Russell barks and scratches at the door. The hills resound with barks and ax blows.

"Can't dump the damn load—lever's froze." Lester tosses aside his ax. He wipes his brow in the crook of his elbow. Brown sweat drips toward his eyes from under his watch cap. He glances up and sees the sun appear from behind a cloud, radiating shafts of light. "Ain't that a picture." He thrusts his chin and cigar skyward.

John looks at the sky. He turns to Lester. "I made a mistake this morning, Mr. Farnum."

"You don't need no wood?"

"It's not that. Please come inside."

John climbs onto the porch and opens the front door. The dog shoots out and pisses on the dump truck's tires.

Lester steps inside, removes his cap. He stares at the exposed rafters, the warped laths. "This what you have to do when you become a Witness?"

"No, we're rebuilding," says John. "This is just temporary."

"But if the world's gonna end... Do houses go to Heaven, too?"

John shakes his head no.

Suddenly, Lester recoils, puts one hand over his heart and points the other toward the stove where the cats are playing tug of war with a bat. "Ain't that a sign?"

The bat comes apart like a rubber toy.

"No, no. We've had dozens of bats in here since we tore out the walls." John turns toward Lester. "I want to tell you that I had no business preaching to you this morning. I was wrong. And I'm sorry."

"Call trying to save a sinner wrong?"

"No, I don't. But I'm not supposed to save sinners. Not yet. If you're interested in saving your soul, you'll have to speak to Mr. Deuthson."

"He the fellow runs the Happy Hour Bar?"

John nods. The cats crunch the tiny white bones. "Now, ain't that loading the dice? Getting people tanked up leads straight to Dooms-day, don't it?" Lester lights his cigar.

"Scripture does not ban the moderate use of alcohol, Lester. We do not encourage drunkenness. That sort of crowd goes elsewhere. But smoking of any kind is strictly forbidden."

"Wouldn't you know it!" Lester plucks the cigar from between his teeth and walks to the door. He tosses the butt across the driveway. He looks up. His mouth opens, his jaw begins to quiver. Slowly, he raises his arm and his finger points toward the rising full moon. "Mr. McAdam, Mr. McAdam! The end of the world, just like you said."

John hurries to the door. A blood red moon is rising above the white-capped mountains. "Lester, the color of the moon doesn't mean a thing."

"It don't? Ain't there something in *Revelation*—about a plague of vermin and a red moon?"

"*Revelation* 7:12," says John. "'And the moon became as blood...'"

"That's it! We got the bat and now the moon. Jeesum, I got to save my family before it's too late."

"But that doesn't occur until the sixth seal, after the earth cracks open, and the sun turns black as sackcloth; after the fifth seal when those slain for the word of God cried out, 'How long, O Lord.'"

Lester is already outside, heaving himself into his truck. He starts the engine, the air brakes explode. The truck bounces down the driveway, then roars away, casting split logs left and right down the road.

While Mary helps Marcia into her coat and hat, Mrs. Dickey, her skirt spotted with paste, climbs down the porch steps and approaches John's window. She leans over. "Marcia was the only little girl without a costume or mask today. I understand about her not taking part in the pledge of allegiance or school prayer, but isn't Halloween just a bit different?"

John kills the engine. He patiently explains that Scripture forbids the celebration of birthdays, holidays, or other festivities not specifically mentioned in the Bible. He says that Scripture is the unalterable word of Jehovah, that it is not meant to be interpreted or modified, even for half an hour. John says he would gladly give up a few Halloweens, Fourths of July, and Christmases for the rewards of the eternal life.

Mrs. Dickey whispers, "That's too bad, Mr. McAdam." She turns and marches up the day care stairs. She sweeps Marcia into her arms. She hugs and rocks the child back and forth. Kicking and twisting, Marcia wriggles out of her grasp and runs to her father, her doll clutched in one of her upraised hands.

The McAdams drive south along the Lower Plain. Thick clouds cover the dark sky, scud against the distant mountains. The air smells of snow. Marcia dances her doll across her lap. John says he must stop at the Kingdom Hall to explain to Mr. Deuthson what happened that afternoon with Lester. Mary pats his arm to encourage him.

Inside the hall, John is greeted by a hundred plastic chairs linked together by steel hooks. John walks lightly, trying to keep his shoes from squeaking on the waxed linoleum floor. He passes behind the lectern where Mr. Deuthson speaks on Sundays. The air under the apse feels thick, dense with Jehovah's presence.

John stops in front of the meeting room door. He unzips his coat; he tucks his shirt into his trousers.

"...He'll make one of our best Witnesses. We haven't seen someone with his skills in many years."

"But his car, Ralph."

"He won't make Service calls in his car," says Mr. Deuthson.

"His house is even worse than his car."

"They are improving the house, gentlemen."

"At his pace, it will take years."

"And he is head-strong, Ralph."

"Yes, he can be impetuous. I agree. But in six months of Bible study he has left the others far behind."

"Ralph, I believe he lives for the Final Trump. That's why he stopped work on his house, why he doesn't tidy the front yard or rake the leaves."

John sees himself barging in with news of Farnum's latest blasphemy.

John knows the Elders will blame him for leading Farnum on. Why did he quote *Revelation*? The Elders will sanction him. They will refuse to baptize him. They will lock him out of the Earthly Paradise forever.

John looked left and right to make sure no one was coming. He dashed to safety on the far side of the lectern, then bolted downstairs to the bathroom. He stood in front of the pure white urinal, his heart beating in his ears like the bell of a fire engine.

Back in the car, he told Mary the Elders were still coming to a decision. Mary praised John's bravery and honesty. John closed his eyes. "Look," said Marcia, pointing across the road. Death and five skeletons were walking into town, dragging their black shiny trick-or-treat bags behind them.

Lit by kerosene lamps and candles, the McAdams' house looked like a giant's jack-o'-lantern gleaming in the middle of the round hills and leafless trees. John and Mary, carrying Marcia, hurried up the driveway. They circled Lester's dump truck. John prayed the lever had thawed enough to dump the load. At the front door they stopped short, peered into the house. In the kitchen, Bessie Farnum worked three large pots, lifting pot lids, stirring the contents with a large wooden spoon. In the playroom, the four Farnum girls were posing in their Halloween masks. Russell slept at their feet, his pink tongue protruding. Lester was in the living room stuffing "Awakes" and "Watchtowers" into the wood stove.

John slammed open the door. He ran into the living room and ripped the Witness literature out of Lester's hands. "There's newspaper for kindling."

"Looked high and low. Couldn't find nothing but these," said Lester, on his knees in front of the stove.

Russell barked nonstop to show he was in charge.

"Soup's on," Bessie yelled. "Girls, wash up, quick."

"Mrs. Farnum, what a surprise," said Mary.

Bessie waved her soup spoon. "Mary, you call me Bessie, and tell me where you hide your soup bowls."

"What's the occasion?" Mary asked, fetching the bowls.

"Didn't that man of yours tell you?"

Mary's face was luminous, but her expression was blank.

Bessie wrapped her arm around Mary's shoulder. "Probably didn't want to upset you, dear."

"What's he done?" Mary asked.

John was shouting in the living room. "It's not for us to decide when Doomsday has arrived, Lester. A red moon means nothing until we're told by the Elders what it means. Do you understand?"

Lester stopped blowing on the sluggish fire. He folded his arms and clenched his teeth around his cigar. "Just wanted to be on the safe side, John. Wouldn't want to see my family left out, would you...?"

"Lester..."

"....My little girls roasted like marshmallows."

"Nobody said the world's coming to an end tonight, Lester."

"I saw them signs."

"It's not for us to call them signs."

"Maybe so, but I figure better safe than sorry."

"Trick or treat!" a chorus shouted behind the front door.

The Farnum girls put on their masks and howled at the ghosts and goblins on the porch. Bessie arrived at the door with candies and cookies bouncing in her outstretched apron. The kids snatched the treats up like starving orphans. When her skirt was empty, Bessie marched into the living room. "Quit your jawing, fellas." She grabbed the men by the arms and dragged them toward the kitchen. "Food's on. We've got beet soup, pork roast, potatoes, corn, and beans."

The Farnum girls and Marcia clambered into their seats at the far end of the table. Bessie ladled out soup while Mary spread a tablecloth and handed out napkins and place settings.

"My gal sure knows how to put on the feed," said Lester. He sat down in his chair and unbuttoned the snaps on both sides of his overalls.

"She's the soul of kindness," said Mary, "but I'm still not sure why you came down."

"Ain't John told you?" Lester said.

"Bessie told me," said Mary, smiling at Lester, "that you saw a red moon and jumped to the wrong conclusion." She frowned at John.

"You think so, too, huh? OK, maybe I was wrong."

"Wouldn't be the first time," said Bessie.

"Let's eat," said Lester, his spoon poised above his soup bowl like a kingfisher ready to dive.

Mary asked John to lead the prayer.

Lester lowered his spoon. The girls giggled. Marcia pressed her chin against her neck and squeezed her hands together until they turned white. John prayed.

"Put in a word to keep that damn lever from freezing up again," said Lester.

"Amen."

"Didn't know where you wanted that load," said Lester. "Otherwise, I would've dumped it."

"Halloooo," someone said from behind the front door.

"Go away," John yelled. "We don't celebrate Halloween here."

"Sorry to bother you," said Mr. Deuthson, opening the door.

"Mr. Deuthson! I didn't know it was you."

"What a pleasant surprise," said Mary.

"I tried to call, but the phone was dead," said Deuthson, glancing at the candles and kerosene lamps as he brushed the snow off his coat.

"Please come in," said Mary.

As Deuthson stepped over the dolls and circled the barking dog, Lester whispered to Bessie, "That's the church Elder. I told you something was up."

Deuthson stared at everyone at the table as if he were memorizing names. Mary quieted Russell with a pat.

"Sit yourself down, Mr. Deuthsin," said Bessie, "there's plenty of chow to go round."

"Might just as well make your last meal a good one—if you know what I mean." Lester winked.

Deuthson turned to John. "I have some good news."

"First the good news, then the bad," Lester whispered to Bessie.

"The Elders decided against sanctioning you, John. They recommend a week of intensive Scriptural study."

John's breath shot out with a whoosh. Mary patted his arm and said, "If we had waited at the Hall, we might have saved you a trip out, Mr. Deuthson."

"I was on my way home anyway, Mary. When were you at the Hall?"

"Never mind," said John.

"Now for the bad news," Lester whispered.

"When did you stop by, Mary?"

John waved his hand as if he were wiping moisture off a window.

"John did this evening, Mr. Deuthson. Don't you remember?" said Mary.

"I saw John this morning, but not this evening." Deuthson turned away from Mary and cast his silver blue eyes on John.

"Sure do beat around the bush," Bessie whispered.

"John, if you stopped at the Hall, why didn't I see you?"

"World's gonna end," Lester said, "and they're dickering over who saw who where and when."

"Mr. Deuthson," John said. "I stopped at the Hall to tell you about some new developments."

"Here we go," said Lester.

"But you were in the middle of your meeting. So I didn't barge in."

Lester groaned noisily. The girls quietly left the table.

"You didn't speak to the Elders?" Mary said.

John shook his head, put his hands together, then shoved them out of sight beneath the tabletop. He looked at Mr. Deuthson like a dog that knows its master is going to shoot it.

Mary folded her arms but tears were already springing into her eyes.

"Were you afraid you'd change our minds?" Deuthson said.

"Maybe he was," Lester said. "Maybe he wasn't. But folks, let's stop splitting the kindling into toothpicks." He stood up and gazed around the table. "Now, what about the signs we saw? We ain't regulars at the church, but we've had Bible learning enough to know a sign when we see one."

Deuthson turned to Lester. "What signs did you see?"

"That's what I came to tell you about, Mr. Deuthson," said John.

"Blood red moon and dead bat is what we saw—saw 'em plain as day."

"And what did John say the signs meant?"

"I didn't say anything, Mr. Deuthson."

"Day of Doom, what else?" Lester said. "What else could they mean?"

"What else, indeed," said Deuthson.

"There, Bessie, I told you! Good thing we brought the kids down. OK, Mr. Deuthson, what do we have to do to get saved? John said we have to confess. Should we confess to you?"

"Didn't John tell you?"

"He said to speak to you."

"Mr. Deuthson," John said, "I can explain exactly what happened. If you'd just give me a minute."

"Who knows how much time we've got. I'm raring to confess right now."

"Just what sins are you in such an uproar to confess, Lester Farnum?" Bessie leaned toward her husband, her jaw set.

"The mortal ones, what else? Avarice, theft, fornication…"

"Who've you been fornicating with?" Bessie yelled, smashing Lester with her huge pink arm.

Ducking the blow, Lester side-swiped the table. The soup sloshed in the bowls; red beet stains spread over the tablecloth.

"You can see where Satan has led you, John."

"Mr. Deuthson, please, let me explain."

Tears overflowed Mary's eyes, burning her cheeks.

"There's nothing to explain, John. But after next Monday's meeting, you can expect more than a week of Scriptural study." Deuthson rose from the table and walked into the playroom where Russell was gnawing on the skull of a naked doll. Deuthson shoved himself into his coat. A witch, Death, and three red devils raced in from the living room. Deuthson reached for his throat. The Farnum girls and Marcia pawed the air, begging for tricks or treats, their fingers wriggling like pink worms. The dog started barking, loud and hard. Frightened by the commotion, a bat crawled out of a crevice in the rafters and began to flit around the room like a piece of shredded shadow. The cats immediately began chasing it back and forth while the girls, screaming and covering their heads, dove for cover under the table.

The bat pendulumed from wall to wall. A cat leaped, its claws four white crescents. The bat twirled sideways, a black pinwheel. The cats pounced, then dragged their victim under the stove.

Buttoning his overcoat, Deuthson turned to John. "And until this matter is settled, you needn't come to work. I'll take over the night shift."

Deuthson opened the front door. From the dark gray sky, fat wet flakes of snow whirled down like dervishes.

"Enough gabbing," said Bessie, "my stomach's as noisy as an empty kettle in a wind storm."

"A-yup, that settles it," said Lester. "If the old boy's talking about work and meetings, the world ain't coming to an end—least-ways not tonight."

"Come and get it, girls," Bessie yelled.

"Say, John," said Lester, "I hate to mention it, but things are tight up to our place, too. Could you write me a check before I dump that load?"

John wept, his head bowed, his long white fingers covering his face. Mary cried with her mouth open, her eyes closed, her head tilted upward at an odd angle.

AFTER THE
REVOLUTION

I

We hit Cambridge at rush hour. Stalled cars and red buses, shimmering in the hot air, fill the streets. I can't park in front of Roxana's building, so I pull into an alley about twenty feet away. A cat sits on a crumpled garbage pail, panting, its teeth showing. Lydia says she'll help unload the car, but she's just trying to be nice. She's been sick. Too sick to drive, but not too sick to read, luckily. She's read six books since we left Minneapolis. I grab a couple of boxes—the Saab's full of them—and kiss her on the lips. Lydia smiles, her face is soft and white, her black curls frame her dark green eyes. She coughs, dry and hard. Her cold's followed us 1,400 miles like a crazy blood-sucking insect. She can't shake it. She's lost weight. She's been working too hard ever since she got her year-long grant to study at Harvard. I lug the books—criticism of James and Poe—into Roxana's building, which hasn't changed much in ten years. Crimson staghorn sumacs surround the apartment house on two sides and neat patches of grass spotted with dog shit line the walks. On the ground floor, a massage parlor and a mountaineering store face each other across the hallway. Roxana still lives three flights up.

"Don't let my cats out!" Roxana yells when I unlock the front door. Roxana's lying on her side in bed, puffing a cloud of smoke toward the ceiling. Two cats are curled up like snails at her feet. She squeezes out a phony smile. "How are you, Stanley?"

"Frazzled. Traffic's fucked up from Connecticut to New Hampshire."

"It's Labor Day weekend." She talks loud like a tourist in a foreign country.

"Just more sop for the masses," I tell her. "Give 'em a three-day-weekend, then work 'em like hell till Thanksgiving."

"Same old Stanley."

"Why change a good thing?"

After looking me over, she shakes her head. "No," she says, "you have changed. I can tell by that sport shirt. Ten years ago you wouldn't have been caught dead in a sport shirt."

"The important things don't change," I say, looking for a spot to put down the boxes.

"What happened to the revolution, Stanley?"

"I brought it home, Roxana. What happened to you?"

Roxana cackles, blows smoke toward the ceiling. "When you heard I was working in Central America, I'll bet you thought I was running guns to some guerrillas." Her laugh turns into a cough. "Not any more. I got my MBA in '76 and went to work for the Consultants Collaborative. I'm teaching businessmen in Latin America how to make mucho pesos." She aims a finger at me as if it were a gun. "These days I get what I want, Stanley."

That's obvious from the way she's outfitted her apartment. It's stuffed with expensive equipment, from the television set and the music center (she's got amplifiers, pre-amps, and two huge Fried speakers, which she's let her cats use as scratching posts) to the handwoven Peruvian rugs on the floors and the framed paintings on the walls. Roxana's changed plenty since our activist days. I put my boxes down on a chair loaded with her clothes and ask her why, if she's working, she's still in bed. Is she working the night shift? Again she laughs, a fresh cigarette bounces between her lips. She tells me how a taxi hit her crossing the street, how she's been flat on her back for a month, how she's going to lose her promotion, her bonus, and her vacation.

Roxana's frosted hair shows the black roots and her eyes are glazed, filled with red veins. She's still got a good figure, though—big tits, thin waist, narrow hips—and she flaunts it, wears a T-shirt and bikini underwear. She says she's refused to travel for her company again until her disk heals. She wonders if we still want to rent out her back rooms.

96

She yells everything she says. It must be the pills she's downing to kill the pain.

I tell her not to worry about us right now, then I walk downstairs to get the rest of the load, thinking about Roxana. She's lost and screwed up despite all the money she says she's earning and even though nowadays she "gets what she wants." Outside, instead of my car, I find two black skid marks stretching from the alley to the street. My car's sitting in the middle of the log-jammed traffic. Lydia's trying to make herself invisible in the passenger seat. Cars slip by slow; drivers look for someone to murder.

I jump down the front steps, run out into the street. I climb into our car. "Stan!" Lydia whispers as I gun the engine. She's white, soaked with a feverish sweat, a vein throbs under the skin on her throat. I shoot back into the alley. "Some person was parked behind the building. I said you'd be down in a minute, but then you didn't come. He pushed me right into the street..." Still shivering with fear, she takes my arm, rubs my hand over her arms and shoulders. I kiss her eyelids and the pulsing vein on her neck. I tell her I'm sorry I took so long; I should have left her the car keys. I don't tell her that her cousin's not the same woman she used to be.

When we finish moving our things into the apartment, we splurge at the Chinese restaurant up the block. The decor's plastic red dragons, the place smells of green tea, but the Szechwan food's spicy hot and fresh, and the cook goes light on the MSG.

Lydia's exhausted, her eyelids droop, but after dinner she listens politely to Roxana's sad story. Roxana talks so loud I can hear every word in our rooms. I dust and vacuum, wet mop the floors. I make our bed and lay out Lydia's robe and toothbrush. Somewhere between unpacking our clothes and sorting them in the bureau, which I've lined with shelf paper, I get the point of Roxana's story. She's suing the taxi company for two and a half million. While I fold our clothes neatly, I wonder what Roxana will do with all that do-re-mi.

After I finish setting up our room, I fetch Lydia. Now the television's blasting and the Rolling Stones are singing "Mother's Little Helper" as if they were in the room. I tell Roxana we've had it, we've got to get some shut eye.

Lydia makes it back to our rooms before she says anything. She closes the door and falls against it. "Can you believe her? We've got to do something about this, Stan. I thought she was going to be traveling eighty percent of the time. Now she's going to be here, flat on her back, all the time. She screams nonstop. We've got to find our own place, Stan."

Lydia's eyes water, her neck throbs. I calm her down, rubbing her back, loosening the tense muscles on her shoulders. I gently work out the knots with my thumb and forefinger. I try to reassure her. "It's going to be OK," I say. "You have to remember rents in Cambridge start at $600 a month. We can't afford an apartment of our own. Not until I find a job. Besides, Roxana's your cousin, and she's my old friend, and she—"

"Stan, she doesn't stop yelling."

"I was going to say, she needs help, Lydia."

I rub her back in long, deep circles, her raven hair a mass of dark lines on the white pillowcase. Slowly Lydia lets go, sinks down into the mattress like a spoon in honey. She sighs, "I suppose if anybody can help her, you can, Stan." She rolls over and kisses me hard. "You're a good, sweet man."

I start kissing her, gentle and slow, the way she likes it. Exhausted, she falls asleep in my arms. The next morning she gets up early. She's feeling much better. She's glad we're in Cambridge. She arms herself with a stack of 3x5 cards and twenty sharpened #2 pencils, wrapped in a rubber band. Off she goes to start work at the Houghton.

2

I figure if somebody you know gets lost, you set them straight. Roxana and I go back twenty years. Once she had her head screwed on right. Now she's out in the woods, living on berries and bark, wandering around in tight circles. She's noisy, uptight, drinks too much, mixes alcohol with her medicine. She follows her doctor's orders (bed rest) for a week, then goes off on a shopping binge. One day she comes home with twenty new books. (Taxis work Harvard Square like sharks, but Roxana lugs the books home herself.) The next day, her aching disk sends her back to bed. She downs pills and booze until the pain subsides.

She eats the same way she rests, in reverse. For days, she starves herself. Then she buys a five pound steak. She carves off a piece, fries it in a skillet, loads it down with Mexican peppers (the kind that make you weep when you sniff them), sour cream and mole sauce. The minute the steak hits the pan and sizzles, her friends arrive. Her friends are like her peppers — they come in all sizes and shapes and make your eyes water. Betty's rich, feels guilty about it, works in a shelter for battered women making beds, mopping up; she lives in a tenement with a Hispanic woman, who locks her out whenever she gets angry. Freddy's afraid he'll get AIDs, so he spends less time in the bars and the baths and more time watching Roxana's television and listening to her gold-plated music system. Maureen flies up from New York Wednesday nights to get away from Herb and to meet her lover. Roxana's buddies eat her food, drink her booze, keep her awake half the night, and leave piles of dishes for me to clean. The cockroaches can't believe their good luck.

By the end of September Lydia and I have settled in. Part of my time I spend looking for a job. Three evenings a week I go down to the shelter attached to the Congregational Church and help out, serving hot food and blankets to the homeless who come in on cold nights. I join the Cambridge chapter of Amnesty International and attend meetings once a week. It's poorly organized, big gesture, little action, just what you'd expect in a college town like Cambridge.

Meanwhile, I've had time to figure out what Roxana needs — three good meals a day, a clean room, rest, and no pills or booze. At the first of the week, I march into her room. "Roxana," I say, "I'm going to make you better."

"You're going to what?" she shouts. She's like a toy that's wound too tight. I can tell from the glaze in her eyes she's been drinking. It can't be two o'clock. By six, she'll be unwound; by ten, blotto.

"You'll see. We'll start off by cooking three solid meals a day."

"You can cook?"

"You bet. But you've got to come to the table; I'm not feeding you in bed."

"What's it going to cost me?"

"Nothing, Roxana. I'll even clean up your room for you."

"Who do you think you are, Albert Schweitzer? If you do a good job, I'll pay you."

There's no sense reminding her of the old days when we ate off the same plate and drank out of the same canteen in the dusty heat in Mississippi, in the cool foggy air in Berkeley.

For breakfast I serve her a glass of fresh-squeezed orange juice, and a bowl of either Oatmeal, Cream of Wheat, or Wheatina, plus two slices of whole wheat toast, a glass of milk. For lunch, we eat salads—leafy lettuces, cukes, tomatoes, mushrooms, cauliflower. If the weather's cool, I start lunch off with a bowl of soup. Supper's the pièce de résistance. I cook mostly out of the *60-Minute Gourmet*: chicken breasts in cream sauce with grapes and curried rice; chicken livers with vinegar and puréed potatoes with zucchini, cherry tomatoes, and garlic; curried shrimp and chicken; lamb kebabs; loin pork chops with apples. Once a week I make a batch of fresh pasta on our pasta machine and bake six loaves of French bread. To make the bread light, I add one cup of pastry flour to every three cups of bread flour; I baste the bread with egg whites to make the crusts crisp.

While she's chewing over the chicken breasts, Roxana's eyes grow big; she smacks her lips. "Where'd you learn how to do this, Stan?" She looks me over as if we had just met.

"Anybody can follow a recipe, Roxana."

"Lydia's a lucky woman," she says. "Let's make a deal. You cook, I'll supply the food. Buy the best and freshest food you can find."

From then on, Roxana throws money at me. For a week's worth of food, she gives me four times more than I need. When I try to give back the change, she tells me I ought to be paid for my time and trouble.

I'm supposed to be working part-time, so I pocket the extra cash and start doing odd jobs for her. Soon she's dreaming up a putz here and there and errands everywhere, and paying me time and a half.

Once I've got her eating habits squared away, I start work on pollution control. In her bedroom, she's got dustballs as big as tumbleweed, blizzards of dust from the hanging rugs, a waxy paste on mirrors, pictures, windows, and the TV picture tube. (Roxana's breath made visible on glass.) There are cigarettes everywhere. A hundred unsmoked cigarettes have rolled under her bed. She's snuffed out cigarettes in the plant pots and on the window sills. Dozens of butts float like drowned men in her empty wine bottles; the ashtrays overflow with ashes, filters, matches; the room is full of scars where she's left her cigarettes burning.

Then there's her clothes and bedding. They need intensive care. Her satin sheets haven't been changed in months. A half-dozen pairs of dirty underwear are stuck at the foot of the bed, along with a cracked diaphragm and a tube of dried up contraceptive jelly. Behind the door, a pile of laundry reaches toward the ceiling like sinners trying to climb out of hell. I stuff the laundry into plastic bags and wash ten loads at the laundromat up the block. While her laundry's in the drier, I go back to the apartment and clean up two months of turds in and around the kitty pan in the living room. I bring back the laundry folded. Before I put it away, I straighten out her bureaus. The teak bureau is stuffed with underwear and blouses, plus a couple of cameras, a miniature dictaphone, flash equipment, earphones, and a portable radio. In the oak bureau, lying around where anyone can see them, are her monthly statements from two checking accounts and a money market fund. She's got eighty grand stashed away, and a dozen stocks. All that and she's still collecting her monthly pay check that's twice as big as Lydia's. I put her clothes away.

It takes a week to dust, mop, and wax the floors; another to wash the filth off the windows. Like my father, who always thought the next Great Depression was around the next corner, I use water, vinegar, and balled-up newspaper. By the end of October, the apartment smells like a spring breeze in May.

"When did you learn to do all this, Stanley?"

"After I quit the factory—two maybe three years ago. I figured the grass-roots movement wasn't going anywhere, so I brought the revolution home. Lydia needed support. It was her tenure year."

"If you keep house full-time, you shouldn't have to work. Housewives don't have to work."

"Don't call me a housewife, Roxana."

"You know what I mean."

"What are you getting at?"

"What I'm getting at," she says, "is if you were a woman, nobody'd expect you to get a job. But since you're a man, there's a double standard. It's not enough you clean, cook, and make the beds, you also have to work."

"College teachers aren't paid like business consultants."

"And I wouldn't take you for granted."

"What's that mean?"

Roxana doesn't answer, she lights a cigarette, tosses the match toward the ashtray.

"You think Lydia does?"

"I do, and I think she doesn't listen to you either."

"Come on, Roxana. I can't count the number of times Lydia has praised me."

Roxana says nothing. She has a coughing fit or maybe she's laughing, I don't know which. The robe she's wearing comes undone. She doesn't hurry to hide what's showing.

3

Thanksgiving dinner for her vulture friends sends Roxana back to the doctor. After dropping her off, I go home, sort laundry, fold clothes, make neat piles of the mess we've churned out since the last time I did the laundry. In Roxana's bureau, the underwear that was caught at the end of her bed looks like it won't pull through. I run across the miniature dictaphone she's pushed to the back of the drawer. I pull it out and turn it on. Roxana's recorded a fight between herself and her boss. Roxana says don't blame me for the latest fuckup; her boss says that's what you said the last time. Roxana tries to keep a level tone; her boss works himself up like a teapot over a hot fire. Pretty quick, he's screaming at one high pitch.

The way I hear the tape, it's a typical case of harassment—male boss taking it out on the female subordinate. When she hears the tape, though, Lydia says, "Listen to her. She's twisting the words around until you can't tell which end is up. But now I know why her back began to hurt a couple of days after the accident."

"What do you mean?"

"She was on the way out, Stan. When the car hit her, she had the excuse she needed to turn a minor injury into a major catastrophe. She knew her company wouldn't fire her when she was in the hospital. They're still paying her. And if she wins the law suit, she'll be sitting pretty for the rest of her life. I'll bet you there's nothing wrong with her, physically. Otherwise, she couldn't carry on the way she does—books from the Square, Thanksgiving dinner for twenty friends. She relapses and runs to the doctor to cover her ass."

I say, "You've been reading too many mystery stories, Lydia," but I'm thinking maybe this is Roxana's idea of "getting what she wants." We used to play scams like that when I was growing up in New York. While we were playing stickball, we'd watch for the right person to drive by. Then Vinnie—the best actor in the gang—would thump the car with a fist and fall on the ground as if he had been hit. Vinnie'd threaten the death penalty for reckless driving; he'd threaten lawsuits, revoked licenses, huge insurance premiums. Finally, he'd accept a one time, cash only settlement, enough money to take care of his broken ankle, his bedridden mother, his sister contemplating a life of sin.

I don't know why, but Lydia's working hard to prove Roxana's pulling the same stunt. It annoys me. Sometime in December, Lydia races into the house, her lips working like a pair of castanets. "She wasn't limping! I swear to God, Stan. I just saw her with my own eyes." Lydia's black hair is wild, her eyes are bloodshot, her lips flecked with froth. I try to calm her down, but she pushes my hands away. She catches her breath and says, "I knew she was faking it. I was walking to the market to get the fish. She was coming out of the liquor store. We were about thirty feet apart. She didn't spot me until she was about ten feet away. She wasn't limping, Stan. She walks as well as I do. But when she saw me—I couldn't believe it—when she saw me she started to limp again. Right in front of me!"

"Maybe she's having one of her better days. Sometimes her back doesn't hurt. That's when she usually goes on a binge. Was she dragging a lot of shit around with her?"

Lydia stares at me. I'm rubbing her hands but she pushes me away. "Why do you always defend her?"

"I don't defend her. I think she's got a problem, Lydia. She's in pain. We don't know what it's like to live with pain, to walk around half-drugged all the time. Her values have gone haywire. You know that. You remember what she was like."

"She was crazy then too, only in a different way."

"You're jealous, Lydia."

"Jealous?" she asks, and she puts a hand in the center of her flat chest. "Are you joking?" Now she waves the hand as if she were brushing away dog-dick gnats. "Why would I be jealous of her? All she talks about is her money. She's alone, unmarried, surrounded by her screwed-up friends. She's flat on her back, and her prospects are dim."

"Not if she wins that law suit," I say.

"What difference would that make to you?"

"Who said it would?"

I hold Lydia at arm's length. She doesn't want to look at me. "What's bothering you, Lydia?"

A finger at a time, her fists unknot. She admits she's having a hard time with her research. She tells me a Poe story, I forget its name. Some guy's wife dies. He loved her, but he soon marries another woman. He hates this woman, but as she begins to die, she turns into the dead woman he once loved.

Something like that. I'm not sure. Lydia puts on her college lecture voice. Her words and her sentences grow longer. She says she knows there's a connection between this story and several stories Henry James wrote, but she can't put it all together.

"Lydia, I'm sorry you're having so much trouble."

She breaks into tears. The harder she's worked, the more intangible everything has gotten. She wipes her wet nose. "Would you read it for me? Tell me what you think."

"Sure," I say, and I pat her on the back.

Roxana flings the front door open. It bangs against the wall; white dust sifts out of the hole the knob has made in the plaster. The cats jump off her bed and run to greet her, tails rising like unfurling flags. "Hello everybody!" She limps into the room.

4

After I read the story, I tell her it's about what it says it's about—if you have a strong enough will, you can bring somebody back from the dead.

"That's what it says it's about," says Lydia.

"That's what you wanted to know."

"But I keep thinking that's the supernatural explanation. What's the psychological explanation?"

"If you have a strong enough will, you can love someone you hate?"

Lydia listens to me, respects my opinions. She tries my idea on for size. It fits for a couple of days, then shrinks in the wash. She can't leave it alone; it's a loose tooth she has to toggle. She's a caged animal walking the same worn path, rubbing the same bar, making the same turn. She goes off early and comes home late. I hardly see her anymore. I'd worry she had a lover, but neither of us screw around. Maybe we look, but we don't touch. Besides, the scholars in the Houghton aren't her type. She likes guys with nice bodies, big shoulders, arms that can carry more than a couple of books at a time. The scholars are too busy working to keep their jobs or get their promotions to start up affairs. If the IRA set off a bomb in the lobby, they'd think it was thunder and keep on scribbling notes on their 3x5 cards.

I demand that we spend some time together. Saturday afternoons between twelve and three, we take walks, no matter how busy she is. Two weeks before Christmas, the weather's warm, but I'm depressed. The CIA's mining harbors, Israel's acting belligerent again, and Lebanon's a raw, stinking wound. Iran and Iraq are closing down the Persian Gulf. In America, we complain if we get stuck in traffic, or our favorite TV show is canceled, or the heat goes off for a couple of hours. In the rest of the world, people live in mud huts and pray to some god who never saves them from starvation, torture, or the firing squad.

We walk down Brattle and Garden, streets lined with houses as old as the country, shaded by ancient mottled sycamores. When we get to the Square, Lydia stops at Petrocelli's for some French torte and cafe au lait, and I start telling her how easy we have it. We don't have to worry whether we're for the right or the left; government troops aren't tromping through town looking for intellectuals or Marxists. We're soft and spoiled. . . .

While Lydia is listening, she looks at her hands. She hardly touches her torte; I have to remind her to eat it. Lydia thinks over what I've said awhile longer, then she gets up and leaves the cafe. Afraid I've depressed her, I pay and hurry after her. "I didn't mean to upset you," I tell her, as she walks up the crowded street toward Mass. Ave.

"You didn't upset me," she says. "I'm thinking."

We enter Harvard Yard and walk past the library toward the Houghton. Inside, she stops in front of the guard, who makes small talk while he checks her purse. He pushes a button that opens the thick, leather-padded doors. We walk into the big hall with the hard-backed chairs, the old musty desks, the ferocious scholars surrounded by space, splitting the short hairs. In the corner, a guy with binoculars for glasses is clacking away at a typewriter. Clouds of dust shimmer in the sunlight shafting through the grimy windows.

I whisper, "Well, what do you think, Lydia?"

She smiles, nods, holds a finger against her lips flecked with confectionery sugar, opens her purse, and pulls out her index cards. "About what?" she asks, hoisting out a dozen sharpened pencils.

I look around. I look at her. I whisper, "About what we were talking about."

"What about it, Stan?" she asks, in her professor's voice.

"I want to know what you think."

She whispers, "I think it's sad, Stan."

"That's it? Sad. Period?"

She sets out her index cards, old ones to the left, new ones to the right. "It's sad you can't change the world, Stan, but you can't. I know it's important, but I don't have time to worry about it." She pulls the rubber band off her pencils. It snaps across her fingers. "Maybe you shouldn't worry about it either."

I raise my voice. "Somebody's got to be concerned. We can't all go around with our noses buried in books."

Scholars perk up, look around. Everybody's suddenly got little frogs caught at the back of their throats. They all make nervous coughing sounds.

Lydia whispers so low I can barely hear her. "If your concern about the world has begun to depress you, Stan, maybe you ought to think about doing something else."

"Come on, Lydia. We're not talking about going back to square one."

"I'm talking about a re-evaluation, Stan. If the state of the world makes you unhappy, maybe you should find another line of work, something that makes you happy."

"Lay off about the job business, will you? I've been looking for a job since we got here. Anyway, Roxana's paying me plenty for the work I do for her."

"For housework, Stan. And errands."

"Don't call it housework."

"You could get a better job if you tried, Stan."

"No job's better than the work I do at the shelter and the Amnesty meetings I'm running. And the work I do for both of you."

Lydia flaps a hand to quiet me down, but I get angrier and talk louder. In the corner, the typist has worked his way down to a clack every couple of seconds. Across from us, a guy pulls his glasses down his nose to get a better look.

"You looking at me?" I ask. "If anybody's doing nothing about world conditions, it's you. Who the hell cares what James thought about Poe? Nobody. Nobody, but you and three other assholes like you. Meanwhile, the whole fucking world's going to get blown to smithereens."

"Would you please quiet down?" someone asks.

"Make me," I yell back.

"That's enough, Stan," Lydia whispers.

"The world's going to hell in a handbasket," I shout, "and you're all farting in the wind."

106

Lydia grabs my arm, I yank it away. The guard comes in, starts moving toward me, tries to look like a bouncer by puffing out his chest; the last thing he bounced was his grandson's rubber ball.

I throw my shoulders back, straighten up. I brush past him on my way out. He totters like a ten pin. I end up in the Square. The sun is almost warm, and the pimps, weirdos, and loonies have crawled out from under their rocks. In the concrete park in front of the Holyoke Center, the street musicians are thumping out sad songs. The tourists pitch money. It's their duty to feed the animals, but they keep their distance. In front of the guitar cases, opened like alligator jaws and studded with coins, a group of hairy-legged women sits as blissful as nuns.

I run into Bailey's up the street, but it takes forever to buy a cone, so I walk around the corner to the International Bookstore. I browse the political science shelves until some faggot starts breathing his perfumed breath on me. I walk home, up Brattle, down Eliot to Mass. Ave. I come out directly across the street from our building where the mountaineering store and the massage parlor share the same front door.

Upstairs, the Rolling Stones' "Under My Thumb" shakes the walls. As usual, I knock on Roxana's door to let her know I'm home. This time, though, she doesn't answer. I push the door open and step into the room. She's lying on her side in bed. "Roxana?" She doesn't answer. An empty jug of wine and a bottle of codeine lie on the floor. I think she's finally mixed herself the brain-killer combination. But then she moans softly and rolls from her side to her back. The satin sheet slides away from her body. I feel like a Boy Scout caught between a blind man and an old lady going in opposite directions at the same intersection. I stand and stare. There's not an ounce of fat on her body. Her skin is smooth and firm. She takes a long, deep breath, then whispers moist and throaty, "Touch me, Stanley." She takes my hand, rubs it slowly over her soft skin. I sink down beside her. She draws my head to her lips, rubs my hand across her tight nipples. She shudders. "Please, Stanley." We kiss, she starts breathing fast. "Stanley. . . ." Then she stops. She looks at me, her eyes misty.

We start kissing again, become a tangle of arms, legs, thighs, and heavy breathing. The music gets loud, blends into one continuous drumbeat, thumping away. We go delirious until I realize she's panting with pain, not passion. "Stanley," she yells, "I've got a spasm. Quick, get me some wine!"

I look everywhere, but there's no wine in the house. I run downstairs. I dash up Mass. Ave. to the liquor store. When I get back to the apartment, Lydia's home, sitting on the edge of Roxana's bed. She says she's tired of working at the Houghton. She's all humble smiles. Roxana grabs the bottle, yanks it open, and gulps down warm Chablis. I check my fly. Lydia waits until Roxana's noisy swallowing subsides, then says, "I finally figured out that Poe story. You were right. Remember what you said?"

The silence sits on us like too much Thanksgiving dinner. I can hardly look at Lydia. "Of course I remember. What do you think?"

"Under My Thumb" starts playing again. I switch to something lighter and turn down the volume.

Lydia lowers her head. "But that's not important." She looks at me. "I'm sorry about today, Stan. I wasn't listening to you. I was preoccupied. I want you to know I think the stuff you're doing for Amnesty International and the shelter is extremely important; the Honeywell sit-ins in Minneapolis were, too. I'm proud you take those things seriously. Even if they don't pay us very much."

Roxana swigs wine from the bottle, tries to hide a smile that creeps out and curls at the corners of her lips.

I don't know what to say.

"I'm sorry I was so selfish," Lydia says. She reaches over and takes my hand, rubs it slowly.

I say, "We were just straightening things up when Roxana got a spasm."

Roxana chokes and splutters on wine.

Beautiful Lydia. She ignores Roxana, glances around. "The room looks great since you started cleaning it up. The whole apartment does."

Then the silence grinds down again like a heavy case of heartburn. The wine sloshes obscenely. There's love juice on Roxana's sheet. My eyes bounce from the dark stain, to Roxana, to Lydia.

"Lydia," says Roxana, "why are you always so condescending when you talk about Stanley's work?"

"I wasn't aware I was being condescending."

"Sure you were. You talk down to him. You say, 'Even though it doesn't pay us very much,' when you know it doesn't pay anything."

"Is that what I said?"

"Would you like to hear?" Roxana reaches under the sheets and pulls out her miniature dictaphone. She clicks it off.

"How long has that been on?" I ask.

"Ever since you came home, Stanley."

A grin sticks itself to my face like a tattoo on a fat man's arm. The cats are curled up and sleeping as if nothing was wrong while outside some ambulance cuts up the street, and the shrill whine of its siren whacks, whacks, whacks against the building.

ALVIN HANDELMAN

was born and brought up in New York City. He has also lived in Providence, Rhode Island, Cambridge, Massachusetts, and in Vermont before settling in Northfield, Minnesota in 1975. Over the years, he has been employed as a librarian, case worker, bank clerk, carpenter, Vista Volunteer, day-care facilitator, woodworker, cameraman, senior editor for a business communications firm, and movie critic, a variety of occupations and interests often reflected in his stories.

Handelman's stories—which have appeared in *Twin Cities, New England Review, John O'Hara Journal, The Lake Street Review,* and *Hellcoat Press*—are tough, hard-edged, and sometimes very, very funny. His lead characters include a fundamentalist minister-in-training, a journalist, a weird family of sex offenders, yuppie inhabitants of a rural New England community, and a college professor who has problems with a pet cat.

Influential in his writings have been the works of several European authors, including Samuel Beckett, Albert Camus, and Franz Kafka. He has also been much attracted to such American writers as Flannery O'Connor, John Gardner, Tim O'Brien and poet Robert Frost. In 1981, Handelman studied with Gardner and O'Brien at Bread Loaf Writers' Conference in Ripton, Vermont. He is currently working on a book about traveling and travelers in Yugoslavia and on a new collection of short stories.